FIRST FLIGHT

Arith executed a little run before he jumped skyward, then his fragile-looking, transparent wings took the first mighty sweep downward. It was the most exhilarating experience I had ever had, and I envied dragonriders anew as Arith's strong wings carried us further aloft.

M'barak must have known how I was feeling, for he turned his head and gave me a wide pleased grin. "Hold on now, Rill, we're going *between*," he yelled.

Then there was blackness, nothingness, and only the knowledge that riders and dragons experienced the same thing daily with no ill effect kept me from screaming in fear.

By Anne McCaffrey
Published by Ballantine Books:

DECISION AT DOONA
DINOSAUR PLANET
DINOSAUR PLANET SURVIVORS
GET OFF THE UNICORN
THE LADY
PEGASUS IN FLIGHT
RESTOREE
THE SHIP WHO SANG
TO RIDE PEGASUS

THE DRAGONRIDERS OF PERN®
Dragonsdawn
Dragonflight
Dragonquest
The White Dragon
Moreta: Dragonlady of Pern
Nerilka's Story
The Renegades of Pern
All the Weyrs of Pern

THE CRYSTAL SINGER BOOKS
Crystal Singer
Killashandra
Crystal Line

Edited by Anne McCaffrey:
Alchemy and Academe

Nerilka's Story

Anne McCaffrey

Illustrations by Edwin Herder

A Del Rey Book

BALLANTINE BOOKS • NEW YORK

THE DRAGONRIDERS OF PERN is a trademark of Anne
McCaffrey. Reg. U.S. Pat. & Tm. Off.

A Del Rey Book
Published by Ballantine Books

Copyright © 1986 by Anne McCaffrey
Illustrations Copyright © 1986 by Edwin Herder

Library of Congress Catalog Card Number: 85-26864

ISBN 0-345-33949-5

Manufactured in the United States of America

First Hardcover Edition: March 1986
First Mass Market Edition : February 1987
Twelfth Printing: March 1993

Cover Art by Edwin Herder

The People

Fort Hold

Nerilka   daughter of Lord Holder
Tolocamp and Lady Pendra

Her brothers and sisters in order of birth:
Campen, Pendora (married),
Mostar, Doral, Theskin,
Silma, Nerilka, Gallen, Jess,
Peth, Amilla, Mercia & Merin
(twins), Kista, Gabin, Mara,
Nia, and Lilla

Munchaun	Nerilka's favorite uncle and Tolocamp's elder brother
Sira	aunt in charge of Weaving
Lucil	aunt in charge of Nursery
Felim	head cook
Barndy	Hold bailiff
Casmodian	main harper
Theng	guard leader
Sim	Nerilka's personal drudge
Garben	a minor holder, Nerilka's suitor
Anella	Tolocamp's second wife

Harper and Healer Halls

Masterhealer Capiam
Masterharper Tirone

Desdra	journeywoman healer studying for her mastery
Master Fortine	Capiam's second in command
Master Brace	Tirone's second in command
Macabir	healer in internment camp

High Hill Hold

| Bestrum | minor holder on Fort/Ruathan border |
| Gana | Bestrum's lady |

Pol	runnerbeast handler
Sal	his brother
Trelbin	High Hill's healer, believed dead

Ruatha Hold

Alessan	newly confirmed Lord Holder of Ruatha
Oklina	his young sister
Tuero	journeyman harper stranded at Ruatha during the plague
Dag	Alessan's chief beasthandler
Fergal	Dag's grandson
Deefer	holder
Lord Leef	Alessan's father, deceased
Suriana	Alessan's wife, deceased, had been Nerilka's foster sister at Misty Hold

Dragonriders at Various Weyrs

Moreta	Weyrwoman of Fort, Orlith's rider
Leri	retired Weyrwoman at Fort, Holth's rider
Falga	Weyrwoman at High Reaches, Tamianth's rider

Bessera	Weyrwoman at High Reaches, Odioth's rider
Kamiana	Weyrwoman at Fort, Pelianth's rider
G'drel	dragonrider at Fort Weyr, bronze Dorianth
B'lerion	dragonrider at High Reaches Weyr, bronze Nabeth
Sh'gall	Weyrleader of Fort Weyr, bronze Kadith
M'tani	Weyrleader of Telgar Weyr, bronze Hogarth
S'peren	dragonrider at Fort Weyr, bronze Clioth
K'lon	dragonrider at Fort Weyr, blue Rogeth
M'barak	dragonrider at Fort Weyr, blue Arith

Others

Ratoshigan	Lord Holder, South Boll
Balfor	Beastcraftmaster elect, Keroon Hold

Prologue

*I*f the reader is unfamiliar with the
series *The Dragonriders of Pern*, certain confusions
may occur. *Nerilka's Story* is an ancillary tale to
Moreta: Dragonlady of Pern, told from the point of
view of one of the minor characters in that novel.

To summarize the background:

Rukbat, in the Sagittarian Sector, was a golden
G-type star. It had five planets, two asteroid belts,
and a stray planet that it had attracted and held
in recent millennia. When men first settled on
Rukbat's third world and called it Pern, they had

taken little notice of the strange planet swinging around its adopted primary in a wildly erratic orbit. For two generations, the colonists gave the bright Red Star little thought—until the path of the wanderer brought it close to its stepsister at perihelion. When such aspects were harmonious and not distorted by conjunctions with other planets in the system, parasitic organisms indigenous to the wandering planet sought to bridge the space gap between their home and the more temperate and hospitable planet. At these times, silver Threads dropped through Pern's skies, destroying anything they touched. The initial losses the colonists suffered were staggering. As a result, during the subsequent struggle to survive and combat the menace, Pern's tenuous contact with the mother planet was broken.

To control the incursions of the dreadful Threads—for the Pernese had cannibalized their transport ships early on and abandoned such technological sophistication as was irrelevant to the pastoral planet—the more resourceful men embarked on a long-term plan. The first phase involved breeding a highly specialized variety of fire-lizard, a life form indigenous to their new world. Men and women with high empathy ratings and some innate telepathic ability were trained to use and preserve the unusual animals. The dragons—named for the mythical Terran beast they resembled—had two valuable characteristics: They could instantaneously travel from one place to another, and after chewing a phosphine-bearing rock, they could emit a flaming gas. Because the dragons could fly, they could intercept and char the Thread in midair before it reached the surface.

It took generations to develop to the fullest the potential of the dragons. The second phase of the proposed defense against the deadly incursions would take even longer. For Thread, a space-traveling mycorrhizoid spore, devoured with mindless voracity all organic matter and, once grounded, burrowed and proliferated with terrifying speed. So a symbiote of the same strain was developed to counter this parasite, and the resulting grub was introduced into the soil of the Southern Continent. It was planned that the dragons would be visible protection, charring Thread while it was still skyborne and protecting the dwellings and the livestock of the colonists. The grub-symbiote would protect vegetation by devouring what Thread managed to evade the dragons' fire.

The originators of the two-stage defense did not allow for change or for hard geological fact. The Southern Continent, though seemingly more attractive than the harsher northern land, proved unstable, and the entire colony was eventually forced to seek refuge from the Threads on the continental shield rock of the north.

On the northern continent the original Fort, Fort Hold, constructed on the eastern face of the Great West Mountain Range, was soon outgrown by the colonists, and its capacious beasthold could not contain the growing numbers of dragons. Another settlement was started slightly to the north, where a great lake had formed near a cave-filled cliff. But Ruatha Hold, too, became overcrowded within a few generations.

Since the Red Star rose in the east, the people of Pern decided to establish a holding in the eastern mountains, provided a suitable cavesite could be found. Only solid rock and metal, which was in distressingly short supply on Pern, were impervious to the burning score of Thread.

The winged, tailed, fire-breathing dragons had by then been bred to a size that required more spacious accommodations than the cliffside holds could provide. The cavepocked cones of extinct volcanoes, one high above the first Fort, the other in the Benden Mountains, proved to be adequate and required only a few improvements to be made habitable.

The dragons and their riders in their high places and the people in their cave holds went about their separate tasks, and each developed habits that became custom, which solidified into tradition as incontrovertible as law. And when a Fall of Thread was imminent—when the Red Star was visible at dawn through the Star Stones erected on the rim of each Weyr—the dragons and their riders mobilized to protect the people of Pern.

Then came an interval of two hundred Turns of the planet Pern around its primary—when the Red Star was at the far end of its erratic orbit, a frozen, lonely captive. No Thread fell on Pern. The inhabitants erased the signs of Thread depredation and grew crops, planted orchards, and thought of reforestation for the slopes denuded by Thread. They even managed to forget that they had once been in great danger of extinction. Then, when the wandering planet returned, the Threads fell again, bringing another fifty years of attack from the skies. Once again the Pernese thanked their ancestors, now many generations removed, for providing the dragons whose fiery breath seared the falling Thread midair.

Dragonkind, too, had prospered during that Interval and had settled in four other locations, following the master plan of interim defense.

Recollections of Earth receded further from Pernese memories with each generation until knowledge of Mankind's origins degenerated into a myth. The significance of the Southern Hemisphere—and the Instructions formulated by the colonial defenders of dragon and grub—became garbled and lost in the more immediate struggle to survive.

By the Sixth Pass of the Red Star, a complicated sociopolitical-economic structure had been developed to deal with the recurrent evil. The six Weyrs, as the old volcanic habitations of the dragonfolk were called, pledged themselves to protect Pern, each Weyr having a geographical section of the Northern Continent literally under its wing. The rest of the population agreed to tithe support to the Weyrs since the dragonmen did not have arable land in their volcanic homes, could not afford to take time away from nurturing their dragons to learn other trades during peacetime, and could not take time away from protecting the planet during Passes.

Settlements, called holds, developed wherever natural caves were found—some, of course, more extensive or strategically placed than others. It took a strong man to exercise control over terrified people during Thread attacks; it took wise administration to conserve victuals when nothing could be safely grown; and it took extraordinary measures to control population and keep it productive and healthy until such time as the menace passed.

Men with special skills in metalworking, weaving, animal husbandry, farming, fishing, and mining formed Crafthalls in each large Hold and looked to one Mastercrafthall where the precepts of the Craft were taught and Craft skills were preserved and guarded from one generation to another. One Lord Holder could not deny the products of the Crafthall situated in his Hold to others, since the Crafts were deemed independent of a Hold affiliation. Each Craftmaster of a Hall owed allegiance to the Master of his particular Craft—an elected office based on proficiency in the Craft and on administrative ability. The Mastercraftsman was responsible for the output of his Halls and the distribution, fair and unprejudiced, of all Craft products on a planetary rather than parochial basis.

Certain rights and privileges accrued to different Leaders of Holds and Masters of Crafts and, naturally, to the dragonriders whom all Pern looked to for protection during the Threadfalls.

It was within the Weyrs that the greatest social revolution took place, for the needs of the dragons took priority over all other considerations. Of the dragons, the gold and green were female, the bronze, brown, and blue male. Of the female dragons, only the golden were fertile; the greens were rendered sterile by the chewing of firestone, which was as well since the sexual proclivities of the small greens would soon have resulted in overpopulation. They were the most agile, however, and invaluable as fighters of Thread, fearless and aggressive. But the price of fertility was inconvenience, and riders of queen dragons carried flamethrowers to char Thread. The blue males were sturdier than their smaller sisters, while the browns and bronzes had the staying power for long, arduous battles against Thread. In theory, the great golden fertile queens were mated with whichever dragon could catch them in their strenuous mating flights. Generally speaking, the bronzes did the honor. Consequently, the rider of the bronze dragon who flew the senior queen of a Weyr became its Leader and had charge of the fighting Wings during a Pass. The rider of the senior queen dragon, however, held the most responsibility for the Weyr during and after a Pass, when it was the Weyrwoman's job to nurture and preserve the dragons, to sustain and improve the Weyr and all its folk. A strong Weyrwoman was as essential to the survival of the Weyr as dragons were to the survival of Pern.

To her fell the task of supplying the Weyr, fostering its children, and Searching for likely candidates from Hall and Hold to pair with the newly hatched dragons. As life in the Weyrs was not only prestigious but easier for women and men alike, Hold and Hall were proud to have their children taken on Search, and boasted of the illustrious members of the bloodline who had become dragonriders.

Now, in the year or Turn of their reckoning 1541, when the Sixth Pass of the Red Star is nearly over, the inhabitants, Lord Holders, Craftmasters, and the Weyrs face a new peril, which threatens them as surely as does Thread.

Chapter I
3.11.1553 Interval

I am not a harper, so do not expect the polished tale. This is a personal history, though, and as accurate as memory can make it: my memory, so the perceptions will be one-sided. No one can challenge the fact that I have lived through a momentous time in Pern's history, a tragic time. I survived the Great Plague, though my heart still grieves for those lost to its virulence, and ever will.

I have, I think, finally adjusted my thinking to a positive attitude toward death. Not even the most abject self-recriminations will breathe life back into the dead long enough to give absolution to the living. Like many another, what I grieve for is what I did *not* do or say to my sisters, now beyond speech or sight or the receipt of my charitable farewell on that day which was the last I saw them.

On that balmy morning, when my father, Lord Tolocamp, my mother, Lady Pendra, and four of my younger sisters set off on their journey to Ruatha Hold and its Gather four days hence, I did not bid them farewell and safe journey. Until common sense reasserted itself, I did, I admit, worry that my lack of charity on that occasion caused their misadventure. But there were plenty of well-wishers that morning, and surely my brother Campen's exhortations would have been a more powerful farewell than any grudgingly given sentiment of mine. For he, at long last, had been left in charge of Fort Hold during my father's absence and he meant to make the most of opportunity. Campen is a fine fellow, despite a lack of any vestige of humor and little sensitivity. There is not a devious bone in his body. As his entire plan was to amaze my father with his industry and efficiency in managing the Hold, it also required my parent's safe return. I could have told poor Campen that all the approval he was likely to receive was a grunt from Father, who would have expected industry and efficiency from his son and heir. With the entire guard com-

plement of Fort Hold, all the cottagers, and the Harper Hall apprentices adding their exuberant presences to the send-off, there were sufficient good wishes to have pleased any wayfarer. No one would have noticed my defection. Except, perhaps, my sharp-eyed sister Amilla, who missed nothing that she might use to her advantage at a later date.

In truth, while I certainly wished them no harm, since Threadfall had been endured the day before with no infestations to ravage the winter fields, I couldn't have wished them merry on their way. For I had been left behind on purpose, and it had been hard indeed to listen to my sisters' prattling about their vain hopes for conquests at the Ruatha Gather and know that the festivities would not include me.

To be excluded in such a peremptory fashion, a flick of my sire's hand to strike me from the travel list, was another insensitive act of judgment. Typical of him when human feelings are concerned—at least typical of his attitudes and judgments until he came back from Ruatha and immured himself in his apartments all those long weeks.

There was no real reason to have excluded me. One more traveler would have made no difference to any of my father's arrangements or discommoded the expedition. Even when I approached my mother and pleaded with her, reminding her that I had undertaken all the disagreeable tasks allotted us girls in the hope of attending Alessan's first Gather, she had been unresponsive. In the throes of that cruel disappointment, I know I lost my case when I blurted out that I had, after all, been fostered with Suriana, Alessan's wife, dead of an unfortunate fall from her wild runnerbeast.

"Then Lord Alessan will scarcely wish to see your face and be reminded of his loss on such an occasion."

"He has never seen my face," I had protested. "But Suriana was my friend. You know that she wrote me many letters from Ruatha. Had she lived to become Lady Holder, I would have been her guest. I know it."

"She is a full Turn in her grave, Nerilka," my mother had reminded me in her coolest voice. "Lord Alessan must choose a new bride."

"You cannot possibly think that my sisters have the slightest chance of attracting Alessan's attention . . ." I began.

"Have some pride, Nerilka. If not for yourself, for your Bloodline," my mother had replied angrily. "Fort is the first Hold, and there isn't a family on Pern that—"

"Wants any of the ugly Fort daughters of this generation. Too bad you married Silma off so quickly. She was the only pretty one of the lot of us."

"Nerilka! I'm shocked! If you were younger, I'd . . ."

Even holding herself erect in anger, Mother still had to look up at me, an attitude which did not endear me further in her eyes.

"Since I'm not, I suppose I shall have to supervise the drudges' bathing once again."

I took a savage satisfaction from the expression on her face, for that had obviously been the very thought in her head for discipline.

"At this time of the cold season, they always benefit from warm water and soapsand. And when you've done that, you will clear the snake traps on the lowest level!" She had waggled her finger under my nose. "I find that lately your attitude leaves much to be desired in a daughter, Nerilka. You are to study a more congenial manner for my return, or I warn you, you will find your privileges curtailed and your duties increased. If you will not abide my authority, I will have no option but to apply to your father for disciplinary action." She dismissed me then, her face still ruddy with controlled anger at my impertinence.

I left her apartments with my head high, but the threat of applying to my father's judgment was not one I wished to challenge. His hand weighed as heavy on the oldest and biggest of us as it did on the youngest.

When I had had a chance to review that interview with my mother, as I ruthlessly sent the drudges into the warm pools and sanded the backs of those whose ablutions were not energetic enough to suit my frame of mind, I regretted my hasty words on several counts. I had probably prejudiced my chance of getting to another Gather for the entire Turn, and I had unnecessarily wounded my mother.

It could not be considered her fault that her daughters were plain. She was a handsome enough woman even now in her fiftieth Turn and despite almost continuous pregnancies which had resulted in nineteen living offspring. Lord Tolocamp was considered a fine-looking man, too, tall and vigorous, certainly virile, for the Fort Hold Horde, as the harper apprentices had nicknamed us, were not his only issue. What galled me excessively was that most of my half-blood half sisters were far prettier than any of the full blood, with the exception of Silma, my next-oldest sister.

Half or full blood, we were all tall and sturdy, an adjective more complimentary to boys than girls, but there it was. I might be a trifle hasty, for my youngest sister, Lilla, at ten Turns had daintier features than we other girls and might well improve. It was positively wasteful that Campen, Mostar, Doral, Theskin, Gallen, and Jess should have black, thick eyelashes where ours were sparse; huge dark eyes while ours were lighter-colored, almost washy; straight fine noses while no one could call mine anything but a beak. They had masses of curly hair. We girls had thick hair; mine reached below my waist when unbraided and was remorselessly black, but it made my skin look sallow. My nearest sisters were cursed with midbrown hair that no herb could brighten. The injustice of our heritage was catastrophic, for plain males would still marry well now that the Pass was ending and Fort's Holder was extending his settlements. But there would be no husbands for plain females.

I had long since discarded the romantic notions of all young girls, or even the hope that my father's position would acquire for me what appearance could not, but I did like to travel. I adored the bustle and uninhibited atmosphere of a Gather. I would so love to have gone to Alessan's first Gather as Lord Holder of Ruatha. I wanted to see, from whatever distance, the man who had captured the love and adoration of Suriana of Misty Hold—Suriana, whose parents had fostered me; Suriana, my dearest friend, who had been effortlessly all that I was not and who had shared the wealth of her friendship unstintingly with me. Alessan could not have grieved more than I for her death, for that event had taken from my life the one life I had valued above my own. To say that part of me had died with Suriana was no exaggeration. We had understood each other as effortlessly as if we had been dragon and rider, would often laugh as one, uttered the observation the other had been about to make, could instantly fathom each other's mood, and shared the same cycle to the minute no matter what distance separated us.

In those happy Turns at Misty Hold, I had even managed to appear prettier in a contentment reflecting Suriana's vividness. Certainly I was braver in her company, urging my runnerbeast after hers on the most dangerous of trails. And I was able to sail in the fiercest wind in the little sloop we took upon the river and sea. Suriana had other attainments, too. She had the sweetest light soprano to which my alto was always in tune. In Fort, my voice goes flat. She could sketch a scene in bold sure strokes; her embroidery was so finely stitched that her mother never feared to give her the gossamer fabrics, and with her to advise me quietly, my stitches improved to the point where later my mother gave me grudging compliments. In one talent only did I surpass Suriana, but not even my healing arts could have mended her broken back. Nor could I, the daughter of Fort Hold, enter the Healer Hall for training. Not when my skills could be employed, free-marked, in the murky stillrooms of Fort Hold.

Now I am appalled at the heedless, uncharitable girl I was that day, unable to swallow disappointment and pride to bid her luckier sisters farewell. For it proved that their luck had run out when they were chosen to attend Ruatha's Gather. But who could have foreseen that, much less the plague, on the bright cold-season day?

We had heard tell of the strange beast rescued by seaholders, for my father had insisted that all his children understand drummer codes. Living so close to the Harper Hall, there was little we did not know of major events occurring across the Northern Continent. Oddly, we were not supposed to talk about the drum messages we heard, lest the information that we could not avoid understanding be indiscreetly repeated. So we all knew about the discovery of the unusual feline at Keroon. It is not surprising, then, that I failed to connect the significance of that message with the later one requiring Master Capiam to diagnose a strange disease afflicting those at Igen. But I anticipate.

And so my parents and my four sisters— Amilla, Mercia, Merin, and Kista—started on their journey through the northern portion of our Hold, where Father meant to check on several holders, to the fateful Ruatha Gather. I who felt she deserved to go remained at home.

Fortunately, I could also remain out of Campen's way, for I was certain he would have special duties for me to perform that would ensure our father's approbation of him. Campen adored delegating duty and thus managed to avoid its tedium, saving his energies to criticize results and expound weighty advices. He is much like our father. Indeed, when Father dies, there will be no skip in the smooth operation of Fort Hold and likely no change ever in the duty roster for me, Nerilka.

The gathering of herbs, roots, and other medicinal plants was a frequent occupation for myself and my sisters, and this duty took precedence over any Campen might have had for me that day. What Campen never twigged was that one did not gather medicinal plants in the cold season, but no one was likely to tell on me. I elected to take Lilla, Nia, Mara, and Gaby with me on my so-called expedition. We did return with early cress and wild onion, and Gaby surprised himself by bringing down a wild wherry with a well-thrown lance. The obvious rewards of our afternoon forced commendation from Campen, who spent the evening meal complaining about the fecklessness of drudges who worked well only under supervision. This was such a frequent complaint of our father's that I raised my eyes from the leg bone I was gnawing to be sure that it was Campen who had spoken.

I do not now recall with what occupation I passed the next few days. Nothing memorable occurred—excepting the summons for Master Capiam, which I heard and so totally disregarded. But knowing would have changed nothing. The fifth day dawned bright and clear, and I had recovered enough from my disappointment by then to hope that the weather at Ruatha was as clement. I knew that my sisters stood no chance of attracting Alessan, but with so many gathering, perhaps some other family might meet my father's requirements for his daughters, and they'd make suitable matches. Particularly now that the Pass was nearly over and Holders could plan expansions. Lord Tolocamp was not the only one to wish to extend his holdings and increase his arable land. If only my father would not be quite so particular in his standard for alliances.

There had been one offer for me, I'm pleased to say. I should not have minded starting a new hold, even if it had meant chipping it out of the cliffside, for I should have been my own mistress. Garben came from the Tillek Bloodline, respectable enough in its lateral descent. I even liked the man, but he and his prospects had not met Father's requirements. Although Garben had flattered me by returning two Turns in a row to repeat his offer—each time with the report of yet another chamber completed in his modest hold— my father had turned him off. Had my opinion been sought, I would have accepted. Amilla had unkindly remarked that I would have accepted anything at that point. She was quite correct, but only because I liked Garben anyway. He was half a head taller than I. That had been five Turns ago.

Suriana had known my situation and my disappointments and had repeatedly expressed the hope that she could talk Lord Leef into permitting me to make an extended visit with her at Ruatha. She was certain that once she was pregnant, he would accede to her request. But Suriana had died, and even that glimmer of hope had been dashed, even as she had been dashed to the ground by the untrained young runner she had been riding. Racing, more likely, I often thought in my bitterest moods. She had confided in me that Alessan had managed to breed some startlingly agile runners when his father had ordered him to produce a sturdier, multipurpose strain. I had only the details that were made public: Suriana had broken her back while riding, and had died without regaining consciousness despite all that the hastily summoned Masterhealer could do. Master Capiam, who was generally willing to discuss medical matters with me, since he knew me to be as competent as my rank allowed me to be, had been markedly silent about the tragedy.

Chapter II

3.11.43 – 1541

*H*eartbreakingly enough, the new
Ruathan tragedy began at precisely the same hour
in which I had learned of Suriana's death, as the
Harper Hall's drum tower vibrated with Capiam's
quarantine command. I was measuring spices for
the kitchen warder, and only the sternest control
kept my hand from trembling and spilling the ex-
pensive spice. Exerting the same control, for the
warder did not understand drum code and I wished
an edible dinner that night, I finished measuring
his requirements, carefully closed the jar, placed it

exactly in its habitual spot, and locked the cabinet. The drum message was being repeated for emphasis by the time I had reached the upper level of the Hold proper, but the second message differed in no particular from the first. I could hear Campen bellowing for explanations from his office as I left the Hold.

Fortunately, so many other people were racing toward the Harper Hall that my indecorous haste went unnoticed. The courtyard of the Hall was filled with anxious apprentices and journeymen, harper and healer. There has always been excellent discipline in the two Crafts, so there was no panic, though some anxiety was evident and many questions circulated.

Yes, there had been calls for Master Capiam from more than just Keroon Beasthold and Igen Sea Hold. Telgar had asked for his presence and counsel; it was rumored he had been taken dragonback to Ista Gather and from there to South Boll at Lord Ratoshigan's express orders, conveyed by no less than Sh'gall, the Fort Weyrleader, on bronze Kadith.

The moment Master Fortine, accompanied by Journeywoman Desdra of the Healer Hall and Masters Brace and Dunegrine of the Harper Hall, appeared on the broad stairs, all fell silent.

"You are naturally anxious about the drum message," Master Fortine began, clearing his throat ostentatiously. He is a good theoretical healer, but has none of the ease that marks the Masterhealer Capiam. Master Fortine raised his voice to an unnecessarily loud, high pitch. "You must realize that Master Capiam would not invoke such emergency procedures without due cause. Would all harpers or healers who attended either Gather present themselves immediately to Journeywoman Desdra in the Small Hall. I will address all healers immediately in the Main Hall, if you would be so kind as to assemble there. Master Brace . . ."

Master Brace stepped forward, adjusting his belt and clearing his own throat. "Master Tirone is from the Hall mediating that dispute in the mines. In accordance with custom, as Senior Master, I assume his authority in this crisis until he has returned to the Hall."

"Hoping that Master Tirone is either caught in the quarantine or dies of the disease . . ." I heard someone mutter nearby. He was immediately shushed by his neighbors, so there would have been no point in my turning to catch out the dissident even if the matter had concerned me more acutely.

Before acceding to the rank of Masterharper, Tirone had once been the tutor to Lord Tolocamp's children, so I knew the man well. He had his faults, but to listen to his rich mellow voice had always been a pleasure no matter what message his words were trying to implant in dull or uninterested minds. A man was never voted to be Master of his Crafthall unless he had more than a glorious baritone voice to recommend him to his fellow Masters. I have heard it said by the disaffected that the only time Tirone has lost a mediation was when he had laryngitis; otherwise, he talked his opponents into surrendering to his decisions.

Naturally the diplomatic Masterharper would take great pains not to offend the Fort Lord Holder despite Craft autonomy, so I had never witnessed that sort of pertinacity in Master Tirone.

What struck me as odd in this moment was that Master Brace should make such an announcement at all—and that Desdra and Fortine represented the healers. Where was Master Capiam? It was totally unlike him to delegate an invidious task. As harpers and healers began to file into the two assembly points, I slipped away from the Hall, not much wiser and with much to worry about.

My lady mother, my four sisters, and my father were now immured at Ruatha. Unworthily, I thought that was another reason why they ought to have taken me. My demise would have been no loss. And I could have been of considerable use as a nurse, really my only talent and mainly unused outside the family. I remonstrated with myself for such reflections and purposefully turned my steps to the lower level of the Hold, where the storerooms were situated.

If this disease had required quarantine, I could occupy myself profitably by checking over supplies. While the Healer Hall had viable stocks of most herbs and medicines, most Holds and Halls were expected to supply their own needs according to their individual requirements. But this situation might require uncommon herbal remedies not normally laid by in sufficient quantity. Campen spotted me, however, and came charging over, huffling as he did when agitated.

"Rill, what's abroad? Did I hear quarantine? Does that mean Father is stuck at Ruatha? What do we do now?" He recalled that if he was acting Lord Holder, he ought not to be requesting advice from any lesser entities, especially his sister. He cleared his throat noisily and poked his chest forward, assuming a stern expression that I found ludicrous. "Have we sufficient fresh herbs for our people?"

"Indeed we do."

"Don't be flippant, Rill. Not at a time like this." He frowned ponderously at me.

"I'm on my way to assess the situation, brother, but I can say without fear of contradiction that our supplies will prove more than adequate for the present emergency."

"Very good, but be sure to give me a written report of supplies on hand." He patted my shoulder as he would his favorite canine and bustled off, huffling as he went. To my jaundiced eye, he appeared unsure as to what he should be doing in this catastrophe.

Sometimes I am appalled at the waste in our storerooms. In spring, summer, and autumn, we gather, preserve, salt, dry, pickle, and store more food than ever Fort Hold could need. Each Turn, despite Mother's conscientious efforts, the oldest is not used first, and gradually the backlog grows. The tunnel snakes and insects take care of that in the darker recesses of the supply caves. We girls often make judicious withdrawals to be smuggled out to needy families, as neither Father nor Mother condone charity, even when the harvests have failed through no fault of the holder. Father and Mother are always saying that it is their ancient duty to supply the entire Hold in time of crisis, but somehow they have never defined "crisis." And we keep increasing the unused and unusable stores.

Of course herbs, properly dried and stored, keep their efficacy for many Turns. The shelves of neat bags and bound stalks, the jars of seeds and salves bulged. Sweatroot, featherfern, all the febrifuges that had been traditional remedies since Records began. Comfrey, aconite, thymus, hissop, ezob: I touched each in turn, knowing we had it in such quantities that Fort Hold could treat every one of the nearly ten thousand inhabitants if necessary. Fellis had been a bumper crop this Turn. Had the land known its future needs? Aconite, too, was in generous supply.

Much relieved by such husbandry, I was about to quit the storeroom when I saw the shelves on which the Hold's medicinal Records were kept—the recipes for compound mixtures and preparations as well as the notations of whichever person dispensed herb, drug, and tonic.

I opened the glowbasket above the reading table and wrestled with the stack to remove the oldest of the Records from the bottom shelf. Perhaps this illness had occurred before in the many long Turns since the Crossing. It was dusty, and pieces of the cover flaked away in my hand. If Mother's assiduous housekeeping had not required it to be dusted off, it was unlikely she would notice the damage. The tome stank with antiquity as I opened it, carefully, not wishing to desecrate it any more than absolutely necessary. I ought to have saved myself the trouble—the ink had faded, leaving only linear splotches on the hide that looked like freckles. I wondered why we bothered to store them anymore. But I could just imagine Mother's reaction if I suggested disposing of these ancestral artifacts.

I compromised by going back to the tome still legibly labeled *Fifth Pass*.

What boring diarists were my ancestors! I was heartily relieved when Sim came to tell me that the head cook earnestly desired my presence. Well, with Mother away, he was likely to apply to me. I held Sim, who was, in any case, not at all eager to return to his labors in the scullery, and quickly penned a note to Journeywoman Desdra, suggesting that Fort Hold's apothecary supplies were at her disposal. I would follow that up as soon as I could, for I doubted that I would be permitted such generosity once Mother had returned to take over the storeroom keys.

I think that was the first moment in which it occurred to me that Lady Pendra would be as vulnerable to this disease as anyone else. A pang of fear or anxiety paralyzed my hand over the script until Sim's throat-clearing roused me. I smiled reassuringly at him. Sim didn't need to be burdened with my silly fears.

"Take this to the Healer Hall. Give it into the hand of Journeywoman Desdra only! Understand? Do not just hand it over to the nearest body in healer colors."

Sim bobbed his head up and down, smiling his vapid smile and murmuring reassurances.

I dealt with the cook, who had just been informed by my brother to prepare for an unspecified quantity of guests. He was at a loss to know what to do, as the evening meal was already being prepared.

"Soup, of course—one of your excellent hearty meat soups, Felim, and a dozen or so of the wherries from the last hunt. They will have hung long enough to be used. Excellent as cold meat, the way you have with seasoning them. More roots, for they, too, can be reheated tastefully. And cheese. We've plenty of cheese."

"For how many?" Felim was too conscientious for his own good. He had been so often chastised by my mother for "wastefulness" that his only defense was showing her the records of how many ate at which meal and what was served them.

"I'll discover that, Felim."

Campen, it appeared, was certain that every nearby holder would be coming to ask his advice about the present emergency, and thus Fort Hold must be prepared to feast the multitude. But the drum message had unequivocally specified a quarantine situation, and I pointed out that the holders, no matter how worried, would be unlikely to disobey that stricture. Those in the home farms might come, since, in effect, they considered themselves part of the main Hold. I forebore to mention that most of these knew a good deal more about managing themselves than did Campen. Still I did not wish to depress him.

I returned to Felim and advised him to increase the portions only by a quarter but to make up additional klah, get a new cheese and more biscuits. Checking the wine stores, I saw there was sufficient in the tuns already broached.

I then went up to the dayroom on the second story, the aunts and other dependents were already aware of the drum reports and highly agitated. I organized them to ready what empty rooms remained into infirmaries. Stuffing clean cases with straw for makeshift pallets would not be too arduous, and they'd feel better for doing something. I caught Uncle Munchaun's eye and we managed to get out into the corridor without being followed.

Munchaun was the oldest of my father's living brothers and my favorite among the pensioners. Until he had been injured in a climbing fall, he had led all hunting parties. He had such great understanding of human frailties, such humor, such humility that I always wondered how my father could have been chosen to Hold, when Munchaun was so much the better human being.

"I saw you coming from the Hall. What's the verdict?"

"Capiam is now a victim of the disease and Desdra tells the healers to treat the symptoms."

He raised his finely curved eyebrows, a wry grin on his face. "So they don't know what they're dealing with, eh?" When I shook my head, he nodded. "I'll start looking through the Records. They must be good for something besides keeping us elderly supernumeraries occupied."

I wanted to deny his self-deprecation, but he

smiled knowingly at me and my protestation would have fallen on deaf ears.

That evening, more of the minor holders came than I had anticipated, as well as all the Crafthall Masters, excepting the Harper and Healer Halls, of course. We had ample for them, and they talked well into the night, discussing contingencies and how to shift supplies from hold to hold without breaking the quarantine.

I poured a last round of klah, though I think only Campen drank any, and retired to my room, where I read the old Record as long as I could keep my eyes open.

Chapter III
3.12.43

*W*hen I heard the drums, I jumped
out of my bed and ran into the corridor where I
could distinguish their pulse. The message was terrifying. Before its echoes had died, another came
in from the south: Ratoshigan demanding assistance from the Healer Hall. It was very early indeed
for the drums to be speaking. I left my door open
as I hastily donned a work tunic and trousers and
belted on the heavy ring of Hold keys. I put on boots,
too, for the soft house shoes were no protection

against the cold stone floors of the lower level, or the roads without.

The drums banged on with more casualties reported at Telgar, Ista, Igen, and South Boll, and more requests for reassurance from distant Holds and Healer Halls. There were volunteers, which was heartening, and offers of assistance from Benden, Lemos, Bitra, Tillek, and High Reaches, places so far untouched by the catastrophe. I found that encouraging, and worthy of the spirit of Pern.

I was halfway across the Field when the first of the coded reports came in from Telgar Weyr: there were dead riders and, because of their deaths, dragon suicides. Passing field workers on their way to the beastholds, I carefully controlled my agitation, nodding and smiling but hastening so that no one would be brash enough to stop me. Or perhaps they did not wish to learn more bad news on top of yesterday's. Hard on the echoes of Telgar's grim news, Ista began citing its report.

Why I had thought that dragonriders would be immune from this disease, I do not know, except that they seemed so invulnerable astride their great beasts, seemingly untouched by the ravages of Thread—though I knew well enough that dragons and riders were often badly scored—and impervious to other minor ailments and anxieties that were visited on lesser folk. Then I recalled that dragonriders often flitted from one Gather to another, and there had been two Gathers on the same day, Ista as well as Ruatha, to lure them from their mountain homes. Two—and plague well advanced in both! Yet Ista was halfway east. How could the disease spring up so quickly in two so distant places?

I hurried on and entered the Harper Hall Court. Everyone here was already up, half of them holding runnerbeasts, saddled and burdened for long trips, their tack in healer colors. Above us the drums continued their grim beatings. From Healer Hall to Hold and Weyr, the messages were sent by Master Fortine. Where then was Master Capiam?

Desdra swung down the shallow steps of the Hall, saddlebags draped on each shoulder and weighing down her hands. Behind her, two more apprentices as laden as she hurried by. The woman looked as if she had not slept, and her face, usually so bland and composed, was etched with strain and impatience, and heavy with anxiety. I edged around the court, hoping to converge on her path as she began to distribute the saddlebags to the mounted men and women.

"No, no change," I heard her say to a journeyman. "The disease must run its course with Capiam as with anyone else. Use these remedies as symptoms warrant. That is the only advice I have now. Listen to the drums. We'll use the emergency codes. Do not send open messages at any time."

She stepped back as the healers urged their runners out of the court, and I had a chance to approach her.

"Journeywoman Desdra."

She swung toward me, not identifying me even as one of the Fort Horde.

"I am Nerilka. If the Hall's supplies are drained by the demand, please come to me—" I emphasized that point by touching hand to chest "—for we've enough to physic half the planet."

"Now, there is no need for concern, Lady Nerilka," she began, mustering a reassuring expression.

"Nonsense." I spoke more sharply than I intended, and then she did look at me and see me. "I know every drum code but the Masterharper's, and can guess at that. He's apparently on the mountain road home." I had her full attention now. "When you need more supplies, ask for me at the Hold. Or if you need another nurse . . ."

Someone called urgently to her, and with a quick nod of apology to me, she walked off. Then the eastern drums began a fresh dispatch of bad news from Keroon. I walked back with the knowledge that hundreds were dying in that tragic Hold, and that four smaller mountain holds did not answer their drumroll.

I was halfway across the Field when I heard

the unmistakable sound of a dragon trumpeting. A chill hand clutched at my innards. What could a dragon be doing at Fort Hold—now? I ran back to the Hall. The massive Hold door was wide open, and Campen stood on the top step, his arms half-raised in astonished disbelief. A small group of anxious Crafthall Masters and two of the nearer minor holders were grouped below him on the steps; all now turned away from Campen and toward the blue dragon who dominated the courtyard. I remember thinking that the dragon was a trifle off-color. Then all else was forgotton as, incredulous, I watched my father striding up the steps, shoving holder and Craftmaster aside.

"There is a quarantine! There is death stalking the land. Did you not hear the message? Are you all deaf that you gather in such numbers? Out! Out! To your homes! Do not quit them for any reasons! Out! Out!"

He shoved the nearest holder down the steps, toward the runnerbeasts which the drudges were only just leading to the stablehold. Two Craftmasters stumbled into each other in order to avoid his flailing arms.

In moments, the courtyard was clear of its visitors, the dust of the precipitous departures already settling on the road.

The blue dragon trumpeted again, adding his own impetus to the scrambling retreat of holder

and Master. Then he leapt skyward, going *between* before he had cleared the Harper Hall tower.

Father turned on us all, for my brothers had come to investigate the unexpected arrival of a dragon.

"Have you run mad to assemble folk? Did none of you pay heed to Capiam's warning? They're dying like flies at Ruatha!"

"Then why are you here, sir?" my rather stupid brother Campen had the gall to ask.

"What did you say?" Father drew himself up like a dragon about to flame, and even Campen drew back from the contained fury in his stance. How Campen escaped a clout I did not then understand.

"But—but—but Capiam said quarantine . . ."

Father tilted his handsome head up, and extended his arms, palms up and outward, to fend off a proximity none of us was at all likely to make.

"I am in quarantine from any of you as of this moment. I shall immure myself in my quarters, and none of you," he said, shaking his heavy forefinger at us, "shall come near me until—" he paused dramatically "—that period is over and I know myself to be clean."

"Is the disease infectious? How contagious is it?" I heard myself asking, because it was important for us to establish that.

"Either way I shall not jeopardize my family."
His expression was so noble I nearly laughed.

Nor did any of my siblings dare ask further
about our mother and sisters.

"All messages are to be slipped under my door.
Food will be left in the hall. That is all."

With that, he motioned us aside and stomped
into the Hold. We could follow his progress across
the Hall and to the stairs by the angry pounding
of his boots on the flagstones. Then a sort of muf-
fled sob broke the spell.

"What of Mother?" Mostar asked, his eyes
wide with anxiety.

"What of Mother indeed!" I said. "Well, let's
not stand here, making a spectacle of ourselves."
I cocked my head toward the roadway where
small groups of cotholders had gathered, attracted first by the dragon's arrival and then our
tableau on the Hold steps.

Of one accord we retired into the Hall. I was
not the only one to glance up at the now closed
door to the first level.

"It isn't fair," Campen began, sitting down
heavily in the nearest chair. I knew that he meant
Father's early return.

"She'd know how to cure us," Gallen said, fear
in his eyes.

"So do I, for she trained me," I said curtly, for
I think I knew then that Mother would not return.
And it was also important for the family not to

panic or give any show of apprehension. "We're a hardy lot, Gallen. You know that. You've never been sick in your life."

"I had the spotted fever."

"We all had that," Mostar said derisively, but the rest of them began to relax.

"He oughtn't to have broken quarantine, though," Theskin said very thoughtfully. "It doesn't set a good example. Alessan ought to have kept him at Ruatha."

I wondered about that, too, although Father can be so overbearing that even Lords older than himself have given way to his wishes. I didn't like to think that Alessan was ineffective, even if he had courteously deferred to Father's wishes. A quarantine was a quarantine!

That night I fell easily into an exhausted sleep but, too restless to sleep well, I awoke very early again. It was so early, in fact, that none of the day staff was about his duties, and I picked up the note tucked under my father's door. I nearly tore it up when I'd read the message. Oh, the stock of febrifuges he wanted, and the wine and food staples were understandable, but he instructed Campen to bring Anella, and "her family" as he put it, into the safety of the Hold. So he would leave my mother and sisters in danger at Ruatha yet ask his oldest son and heir to bring his mistress to safety? And the two children he had sired on her.

Oh, it was no scandal really. Mother had always ignored the matter. She'd had practice over the Turns, and indeed once I had overheard her say to one of the aunts that relief now and then from his attentions was welcome. But I didn't like Anella. She simpered, she clung, and if Father couldn't pretend interest in her, she was quite as happy on Mostar's arm. Indeed, I think she hoped to be wed to my brother. I longed to tell her that Mostar had other ideas. Still, I wondered if her last son was my father's issue or Mostar's.

I chided myself for such snide thoughts. At least the child had a strong family resemblance. With my belt knife, I separated the slip of hide into its two messages and slid Campen's portion under his door. I bore the discreet half down to the kitchen where sleepy drudges were folding up their pallets before starting their chores. My presence provoked tentative smiles and some apprehension, so I smiled reassurances and told the brightest of the lot what to put on Lord Tolocamp's morning tray.

Campen met me in the Hall, distractedly waving his portion of our father's orders. "What am I to do about this, Rill? I can hardly ride out of the Hold proper and bring her back in broad daylight."

"Bring her in from the fire-heights. No one'll be looking there today."

"I don't like it, Rill. I just don't like it."

"When have our likes or dislikes ever mattered, Campen?"

Anxious to get out of range of his querulous confusion, I went off to inspect the Nurseries on the southern side of the level. Here, at least, was an island of serenity—well, as serene as twenty-nine babes and toddlers can be. The girls were going about their routine tasks under the watchful gaze of Aunt Lucil and her assistants. With all the babble there, they would not have heard the drums clearly enough to be worried yet. Since the Nursery had its own small kitchen, I would have to remember to have them close off their section if Fort Hold did surrender to the disease. And I must also remember to have additional supplies sent up—just to be on the safe side.

I checked on the laundry and linen stores and suggested to the Wash Aunt that today, being sunny and not too chill, was an excellent day to do a major wash. She was a good person, but tended to procrastinate out of a mistaken notion that her drudges were woefully overworked. I knew Mother always had to give her a push to get started. I didn't like to think that I was usurping any of my mother's duties, even on a temporary basis, but we might be in need of every length of clean linen ever woven in the Hold.

The weavers, when I arrived in the Loft cots, were diligently applying themselves to their shuttles. One great roll of the sturdy mixed yarns, on which my mother prided herself, was just being clipped free of the woof. Aunt Sira greeted me with her usual cool, contained manner. Although she must have heard some of the drum messages over the clack of heddle and shuttle, she made no comment on the world outside.

I had a late breakfast in the little room on the first sublevel, which Mother called her "office," as grateful as she must often have been for this retreat. Still the drums rolled, acknowledging and then passing on the dire tidings. One didn't hear it only once, sad to say, but several times. I winced the fourth time Keroon's code came through, and hummed loudly to keep the latest message from adding to the misery already in my heart. Ruatha was close by. Why had we no messages from them, no reassurance from my mother and my sisters?

A knock on the door interrupted these anxieties, and I was almost glad to learn that Campen awaited me on the first story. Halfway up the stairs, I realized that he must have returned with Anella and that, if he was on the first story, she was expecting to have guest quarters. I myself would have put her on the inner corridor of the fifth story. But the apartment at the end of the first story was more than appropriate for her. There was no way that I would accommodate her in my mother's suite, with its convenient access to Father's sleeping room. My father was, after all, in isolation, and my mother was alive in Ruatha.

Anella had obeyed Tolocamp's instruction to the letter. She had brought not only her two babies, but her mother, father, three younger brothers, and six of the frailer of her family dependents. How they managed to climb the fire-heights I did not inquire, but two of them looked about to collapse. They could go to the upper stories and be attended by our own elderlies. Anella pouted a bit at being assigned rooms so far from Tolocamp, but neither Campen nor I paid any attention to her remarks or to those of her shrewish mother. I was just relieved that the entire hold had not descended on us. I suspected the older two brothers had more sense than to chance their arms on their pert sister's prospects. Although I felt Anella ought to be well able to care for her children, I did assign her two servants, one from the Nursery level and a general. I wished to have no complaints from my father about her reception or quarters. Any guest would have had as much courtesy from me. But I didn't have to like it.

Then I sped down to the kitchens to discuss the day with Felim. He needed only to be told he was doing splendidly. The kitchens are always the worst places for rumor and gossip. Fortunately, no one there understood the coded messages, although they must have recognized that the drum tower was unusually busy. Sometimes one knows the drums are relaying good news, happy tidings. The beat seems brighter, higher-pitched, as if the very skins are singing with pleasure at their work. So if I fancied that the drums were weeping today, who could blame me?

Toward evening, mistakes were made in the messages relayed as weary drummer arms faltered in the beat. I was forced to endure repetitions—despairing pleas from Keroon and Telgar for healers to replace those who had died of the disease they tried to cure. I put plugs in my ears so that I could sleep. Even so, my eardrums seemed to echo the pulse of the day's grievous news.

Chapter IV
3.14.43

*O*ne of the plugs fell out during my restless sleep, so I heard the drums all too clearly that morning when they beat out the news of my mother's death, and then the deaths of my sisters. I dressed and went to comfort Lilla, Nia, and Mara. Gabin crept in, his face reddened with the effort not to cry in public. He howled as he buried his head in my shoulder. And I cried, too. For my sisters and for myself who had not wished them a safe and happy journey.

My brothers, all but Campen, sought us out

during the morning and so we had the luxury of private grief. I wonder if any of us hoped that Tolocamp would fall ill of the disease he had left our mother and sisters to die from.

When a messenger from Desdra found me, I welcomed him as an excuse to leave the sorrow-filled room. I could have gone down the back stairs to the stores to fill Desdra's request for supplies, but I led the man through the main corridor. Clearly I heard my father's vigorous voice calling out the window, and I saw Anella lurking just round the first bend in the corridor. Quick as a snake, she scuttled away, but the gloating smirk on her face provoked me past indifference to active dislike and disgust of her.

The healer apprentice was hard-pressed to keep up with me as I whipped down the spiral stairs to the lower levels. When I piled sack upon sack of the herbs and root medicines that Desdra had listed, he protested that he wouldn't be able to lug so much to the Healer Hall. I summoned a drudge, my voice almost a shriek, and the scared Sim rushed in answer, his eyes round with fear that he had somehow forgotten something important.

Controlling myself, I apologized to the healer for overburdening him. I would have merely ordered a second drudge to assist Sim and the healer, but as I entered the kitchen passage, I caught sight of Anella sweeping down the steps, beckoning imperiously to Felim. I knew that if I entered the main kitchen and saw that smug little lay-aback playing Lady Holder, I would rue the outcome. Instead, I left by the side door with healer and drudge. The chill afternoon air enveloped and cooled me, though I set a brisk pace for my companions.

The Harper Hall was in an uproar when I got there, alive with shouts and cries of joy. I couldn't imagine what occasioned such joy, but it was contagious and I smiled without knowing why, just relieved to hear some happiness. Then the voices became separated and an unmistakable baritone rang clearly.

"Fog caught me between holds, friends," Master Tirone was saying in clarion tones. "And a lame runner. I caught a fresh mount from a pasture and was proceeding on when I heard the first drum message. I came on apace, I can tell you, and never stopped for sleep or food. I'll apologize for borrowing the runners later, when the drums are not so hot with important messages." The sly hint of laughter in his voice was rewarded by chuckles from the other harpers. "It was shorter to take the back route by then, so how was I to know Lord Tolocamp had set up guards to prevent any of us entering or leaving?" That was the first I'd heard of my father's precautions. Master Tirone's voice dropped to a more confidential tone. "Now, what's this about an internment camp for healer or harper trying to contact his Hall? How are we supposed to work with such a foolish restriction on movement?"

The healer eyed me with some consternation, for this smacked of criticism of the Lord Holder. I could not in conscience show any trace of my growing disgust, disillusionment, and distrust of my sire. And obviously I should not have over-heard such sentiment.

Then Desdra herself appeared from the far side of the Hall court, her face lighting with relief as she saw how burdened we were. "Lady Nerilka, I only asked for interim supplies."

"I recommend that you take as much as you can get before I am no longer in a position to help."

She did not question me, but I saw her eyes accept my words and the implications of my tone.

"I renew my offer to nurse the sick, wherever and whoever they might be," I said as firmly as I could as she took the sacks from my arms.

"You must take your mother's place here dur-ing this emergency, Lady Nerilka," she said, her voice low and kind, her deep-set and expressive eyes conveying her sympathy and condolences. I had once thought the journeywoman too pas-sive a practitioner, her manner too detached, but I had misjudged her. How could I tell her, now, that she mistook my measure and circumstances? Or had such a trivial matter as Anella's arrival not percolated through to the two Halls?

"How is Master Capiam?" I asked, before she could turn away.

"He has nearly completed the course of the disease." Desdra's voice rippled with wry humor, and I detected a twinkle in her eyes. "He's too ornery to die, and determined to find a cure for this plague. Thank you, Lady Nerilka."

Our brief exchange had outlasted the audible conversations from the Harper Hall, so there was nothing for me to do but retrace my steps out of the court, with Sim trotting behind me. Poor Sim. I forget he has short legs and cannot match my long stride.

"Sim, where is this internment camp of Lord Tolocamp's?" I sought any excuse to avoid returning to the Hold for a little while. My anger was too sharp, my grief too fresh, my self-discipline nonexistent.

Sim pointed to his right, where the great road south dips down into a small valley through a copse of trees. I walked far enough down the broad roadway to have an uninterrupted view, and saw guards pacing the arbitrary boundaries.

"Are there many wayfarers halted there?"

Sim nodded, his eyes frightened. "Harper and healer, all only trying to get back to their Halls. And a few of the holdless. We always have them coming along. But there'll be sick ones, soon.

Wanting help from the Healer Hall. What'll they do? They got a right to healing."

So they did. Even my mother was—had been—generous to the holdless.

"Do the guards allow anyone into the valley?"

Sim nodded. "But not back out again."

"Who's the guard leader?"

"Theng, far as I know."

Even Theng could be got round if it was done the right way. He enjoyed a bottle of wine, and while he was drinking he could pretend not to see past the end of the flask. Harper and healer refused access to their Halls? My father was foolish as well as frightened. And hypocritical when he, himself, returning from a disease-ridden Hold, placed his own people at jeopardy by his very presence. Well, that didn't mean that I had to be foolish, too. I knew my duty to the Halls—hadn't my father drilled it into me? And I might need their charity before the end of these terrible days. I would speak to Felim, and to Theng.

As I walked back up to the Hold, I saw a figure in a first story window. My father? Yes, that was his window, and he was watching Sim and me. Sim he wouldn't distinguish from any other drudge wearing Hold livery, but just how keen was his long sight? And what would it matter if he identified me? It would probably be the first time he had. I strode on, proud and careless. But

I did take the side entrance into the kitchens. I had to speak to Felim, didn't I?

"What am I to do now, Lady Nerilka?" the cook began before I could ask him to save the broken meats for the interned men. "She came down with orders for all kinds of foods that I know Lady Pendra would not condone—" And then he burst into tears again, blotting his eyes and face with the rag he always had hanging out of his apron waist. "She was stern, Lady Pendra, but she was fair. A man knew he had only to keep to her standards and there'd be no complaint."

"What did Anella want?"

"She said she was to order Hold matters now. And I was to prepare broth for her children, whose stomachs are delicate; and there are to be confections with every meal, for her parents desire sweets; and roasts midday and evening. Lady Nerilka, you know that isn't possible." Tears streamed down his cheeks again as he shrugged. "Must I take orders from her now?"

"I'll find out, Felim. Proceed with the plans we made this morning. Not even for Anella can we alter an established routine in one day."

Then I asked him to save what he could from the evening meal, for delivery to Theng.

"I took the liberty of sending the broken meats last night, Lady Nerilka. As your lady mother would have done. Oh, oh, she was fair, she was fair. . . ." He buried his face once more in his napkin.

Felim was fair, too, I thought, trying to keep my mind off my mother. Thinking of Anella helped. That little lay-aback, coming in here and thinking she could just take over a Hold the size of Fort and run it as if it were exactly like the backhills midden from which she'd come! The thought of the chaos that would shortly result at such inexpert hands gave me a perverse delight. Little did Anella know of real management, and if she wished to keep my father content, she'd better learn. Whatever had made her think that just because Lady Pendra was dead, she was to step into her shoes, just as she had taken her bed partner? Unless . . .

Once again I encountered a distressed Campen in the front hall. My brother's face was suffused with blood and his features contorted with dismay. Doral, Mostar, and Theskin, who were deep in low conversation with him, wore the same expression.

"Isn't there anything we can *do*?" Theskin was demanding, his fingers clenching and unclenching on the hilt of his belt knife.

Doral was slamming one fist into the other palm. "Nerilka, where have you been? Do you know what has happened?"

"Anella's moving in."

"Father has had her transferred into Mother's

rooms. Already!" There was no doubt of the out-rage that Campen and the others felt. "He's look-ing for you, Rill, demanding to know where you've been all day, what you were doing at the internment camp—and whatever possessed you to go there?"

"To find out if it existed at all," I replied, bitterly ignoring the other questions. "When?"

"That was our early morning task," Theskin replied, indicating that Doral had assisted. "Set-ting the guard and drawing up the watch rosters. Now this! Could he not wait a decent interval?"

"He may come down with the illness and have lost a last chance to enjoy his few remaining hours!"

"*Nerilka!*" Campen was appalled at my irrev-erence, but Theskin and Doral guffawed.

"She may have the answer, you know, Campie lad," Theskin said. "Our sire has ever liked his little pleasures."

"Theskin, that is enough!" Campen remem-bered to lower his voice, but the intensity of his reprimand made up for the lack of volume.

Theskin shrugged. "I'm off. Checking the guard! I'll be back for my dinner. Wouldn't miss that for the world!" He winked at me, tugged Doral by the arm, and they went off, leaving me with Campen.

But I had no wish for a continued lecture on my shortcomings. "Watch out, Campen. She has two sons, you know, and we could all be booted to the upper stories!"

Patently this had not occurred to my eldest brother. As he struggled with the possibility, I made it safely to my snug little inside room.

That evening's meal was one I do not remember eating, certainly not enjoying. Our dead mother had made courtesy in us such an instinctive reaction that we could not, any of us, be impolite despite that night's provocation. I had delayed my descent to the Main Hall, so I was rather surprised to find so many of our relations from the second story. The great tables were set up; even my father's chair sat in place on the dais. Anella had been busy.

"Were you invited?" I asked Uncle Munchaun when he sauntered over to me.

"No, but she'd not know our ways, would she?"

One could count on Uncle Munchaun, not to mention the others, to sense a situation and make sure to witness it firsthand.

"I fear I've found nothing of value in my reading thus far," Uncle continued smoothly. "I've set others to the task, as well. Any word from the Halls? I understand you were there today."

I ignored the thrust. "Master Tirone has returned from that mediation. By the mountain trail."

"Then he missed the additions to our Hold?"

48

"He may have. Certainly he missed the guards."

"I almost wish he hadn't," Uncle murmured, a gleam in his eyes. Then he touched my arm warningly and I turned to see Anella, followed by her parents, sweeping into the Great Hall.

Her grand entrance was spoiled by her flaming cheeks and her father's stumbling pace. The man had not been drunk, I was later informed, but had a crippled foot. But I was in no mood to be charitable or compassionate. He, at least, had the grace to look embarrassed throughout the next few minutes.

Anella, dressed in a heavily embroidered gown totally unsuitable for the mourning of the Hold or for a family dinner, mounted the three steps to the dais and walked firmly to my mother's chair. Uncle Munchaun's hand restrained me now.

"Lord Tolocamp wishes me to read this message to you." Her voice was strident in her effort to be heard and to project her new authority. She unrolled the message and held it up in front of her eyes, which bulged unbecomingly as she shouted at us.

"I, Lord Tolocamp, quarantined from active participation in the conduct of Fort Hold in these unsettled days, appoint and deputize Lady Anella as Lady Holder to ensure the management of the Hold until such time as our desired union can be

publicly celebrated. My son, Campen, will actively discharge under my direction any duties required of the Lord Holder until such time as I am no longer immured.

"I solemnly charge all of you, under pain of disgrace and exile, to observe the quarantine of this Hold, and to refrain from contact with any others until such time as Master Capiam, or his delegate Masterhealer, rescinds the quarantine restrictions. I require obedience to all restrictions made by me to ensure the safety and health of Fort, Pern's first and largest Hold. Obey and we prosper. Deny and we fall."

She turned the sheet toward us and pointed to the end. "His signature and ring mark are here to be verified." Then she insulted us again. "He charges me to discover which of you ventured perilously close to the internment camp today." Her bulging eyes swept the lot of us.

Just as I stepped forward, so did Peth, Jess, Nia, and Gabin.

"Do not anger me," Anella cried. "Lord Tolocamp only told me about one of you."

"We all must have had a look at one time or another," said Jess, speaking out before I could gather my wits. "I've never seen an internment camp."

"Do you not understand? There are sick people there!" Anella's face turned pale with fright. "If you catch the plague, you will infect the rest of us before you die."

"Just like our Lord Holder," came a voice from somewhere in her audience.

"Who said that? Who spoke so vilely?"

There was no answer, only a shifting of boots on the flagstones. Even I could not identify the speaker—to congratulate him, or her. My private wager would fall on Theskin.

"I will know who spoke!" Anella ranted on a bit more, but she would never learn the answer, having shattered any chance she might have had of gaining the trust and confidence of those in the Hall that night. "Lord Tolocamp will hear of the snake at his bosom!"

She glared about the Hall one last time, then yanked at the heavily carved chair that my mother had filled so adequately. She was not strong enough to shift it, and a twitter greeted her attempt. Her mother signaled peremptorily to a drudge to assist her daughter. When Anella finally seated herself, her mother sat down beside her, the husband on her left. Those of us who ought to have taken our places on the dais declined to do so, and with a bit of angling, all were accommodated at the trestle tables.

"Where are Lord Tolocamp's children?" she demanded when we were arranged. "Campen!" She pointed at him, for him she knew by sight. "Theskin, Doral, Gallen. Assume your places."

She paused briefly; I could see her eyes blinking and an irritated twitch to her mouth. "Nalka? Is she not the oldest living daughter?"

Uncle Munchaun nudged me. "You'd best go, Rill, even misnamed, for your father will know if you insult her so publicly."

I knew he was right. As I rose, I saw Anella's mother murmur something to her.

"And there is a harper in this Hold, is there not? We honor the harper."

Casmodian rose, bowed, and managed a smile.

"Why did you seat yourselves below?" she demanded as Campen and Theskin mounted the dais steps.

"With all due respect, Lady Anella," Theskin said with a wry smile, "we thought your family would require the seating here."

Though courteously spoken, Theskin's words were nonetheless a gibe, and she was not too dense to know it, even if she had no adequate retort. No one mentioned that she had not named all of Tolocamp's surviving mature children, so Peth, Jess, and Gabin made a merrier meal than we others did.

Bravely, Casmodian sat next to the father. I think they were the only two to converse that evening at the head table. I know I tasted nothing of even the little food I forced myself to eat. Unfortunately, now I had time to think of all I had *not* done for my mother, of my uncharitable absence from the last moments my sisters had had at Fort Hold. I seethed, too, with fury at the usurper and vowed that I would not lift a hand to assist her in her new role. How convenient that she couldn't even remember my name properly. If I judged the temper of the Hall correctly, she would have no help from anyone, even in such a small matter as the correct nomenclature of Lord Tolocamp's children.

I drank more wine that evening than is my custom—or perhaps it was because I also ate so little. It was enough to finish the meal and slip from the Hall to the kitchens, to be sure that this new Lady Holder had not countermanded my order about the broken meats. Then, by the back stairs, I sought my own room and the solace of sleep.

Chapter V

3.15.43

*T*he drums woke me at dawn, for in my giddiness I had forgotten to plug my ears. Then the message woke me up completely—Twelve Wings had flown Thread at Igen and all was well.

How could twelve Wings have flown out of Igen Weyr when half the dragonriders were ill of the plague and the Weyr had already suffered deaths? They could not have mounted more than nine Wings if their casualties had been accurately reported, and there would be no advantage to prevaricate at this terrible moment.

I rose and dressed, then descended to the kitchens to surprise the drudges brewing the first of the many urns of klah. Its aromatic smell was a restorative all by itself, and the first fragrant cup was the best one of any day, heartening me all the more in my grief and dismay. I was stirring the porridge when Felim appeared, his face first brightening, then falling into a suitably lugubrious expression as he advanced on me.

"I was obliged to send basketsful of untouched food to the camps, Lady Nerilka. Wasn't the dinner well enough?"

"Few of us had the heart to eat, Felim. It is no insult to you."

"*She* complained that I did not offer sufficient choice of sweets," he told me, offended. "Has she any idea of the handicaps under which I labor? I cannot chop and change midday. There isn't a single apprentice or journeyman able to provide a choice of sweets on an hour's notice in such quantities as are needed in the Hall these days."

I murmured phrases to soothe his damaged self-esteem, more out of habit than a desire to redeem Anella in his eyes. A disgruntled cook could cause real problems in a Hold the size of Fort. Let Anella learn by her mistakes, and discover just how much hard work it was to be Lady Holder.

It was then that I realized the truth of her announcement: She was Lady Holder, and due all the courtesies and honors that had been my mother's. Well, there were certain private possessions of my mother's that would not fall into her hands. I said a few pacifying words to Felim, to ensure a decently cooked meal this evening, and rushed to my mother's office on the sublevel.

There I quickly removed all her private journals, her notes about this personality and that worker—we girls had long known her to jog her memory by these entries, and had done our best not to figure in them very often. They would be invaluable reading to Anella and hideously embarrassing to us, not only to have our childhood peccadilloes revealed, but also the problems of the second-story occupants. Mother had some gems and jewelry that were hers in her own right, not Hold adornments, which should by rights be divided among the surviving daughters. I doubted Anella's probity in distributing them, so I chose to undertake that task as well.

If Anella thought these things had been removed, she might search for them, so I hurried along the back passages to the stores and hid the two sacks of journals and the small parcel of jewelry on the top of a dusty shelf. Anella was hands shorter than I.

I was on my way back when Sim intercepted me.

"Lady Nerilka, *she* is asking for a Lady Nalka."

"Is she? Well, there isn't one in the Hold, is there?"

Sim blinked, confused. "Doesn't she mean you, lady?"

"She may indeed, but until she learns to call me by my proper name, I am in no way obliged to answer, am I, Sim?"

"Not if you say so, Lady Nerilka."

"So return to her, Sim, and say you cannot find Lady Nalka in the Hold."

"Is that what I do?"

"That is what you do."

He lumbered off, muttering under his breath about not finding Lady Nalka—any Lady Nalka—in the Hold. That is what he was to say. No Lady Nalka in the Hold.

I crossed the yard to the Harper Hall. Anella might have many things on her mind more important than the pharmaceutical stores, but eventually someone would inform her that it was Lady Nerilka whom she required. And she surely would tell my father of my insolence. When he emerged from his isolation, I had no doubt that he would deliver a thorough and painful chastisement. I might as well merit every blow. Meanwhile, it was my right to dispense those medicinal supplies as required, and I was determined that the healers would have full benefit of them.

I was directed to the Hall kitchens by a cheerful young apprentice and made my way there, reflecting that I seemed to be spending a lot more time in kitchens these days.

"I'll need the glass bottles sterilized, and that means fifteen minutes in water at the rolling boil and no cheating on the sands," Desdra was saying to the journeyman. "Now, I'll—Lady Nerilka!" There was about Desdra a buoyancy that had been absent the previous day.

"Master Capiam is better?"

"Himself again, I'm glad to say. Not everyone who gets the plague needs to die of it. Anyone ill in Fort Hold?"

"If you mean my sire, he keeps to his apartments but is well enough to issue orders."

"So I heard." Desdra's wry smile informed me that she found the change tasteless.

"While I am still in charge of the pharmacy, what are your needs?"

Desdra had turned to watch the journeyman, her mind clearly on more urgent matters. She looked back at me with a smile, however. "Can you decoct, infuse, and blend?"

"I supply all our medicinal needs."

"Then prepare a cough syrup, tussilago by preference. Here, let me give you the recipe that I have found efficacious." She had a scrap of hide in her hand, a charcoal stick in the other; hastily, but legibly, she scrawled measurements and ingredients. "Don't balk at adding numbweed— that is the only thing that depresses the terrible racking cough." Then she consulted another list in her hand. She was distracted by my presence. "And has your mother—oh, I beg your pardon." She touched my hand in apology, her eyes troubled to have caused me pain. "Have you a restorative soup? We shall need kettles of restorative soups."

I thought of Felim's reaction to yet another bizarre request, but the small night hearth could be used, and all kinds of scraps go into the soup pot. The last place Anella would think to find me would be in the hot, small, inner kitchen.

"Cook, cool it into jelly. It'll transport better that way." She had one eye on the sands that were only grains away from her fifteen-minutes-at-the-rolling-boil.

I left her to her task, hoping it bode well. There was a suppressed excitement about Desdra that could not be due entirely to the Master Harper's recovery. Was she brewing a cure?

Fortunately it took all day to concoct both the restorative soup and Desdra's cough syrup. The tussilago really did numb the lining of the throat. I improved the taste with a harmless flavoring and filled two demijohns with the mixture, reserving a large flask for Hold use, should it be required. I made a note of the syrup in the Record.

When Sim and I brought the products of my day's labors over to the Hall, the air of suppressed excitement that I had noted in Desdra was now rampant, but I could find out nothing from the journeyman who took syrup and soup from me. He thanked me profusely enough, but plainly had other tasks pending.

It was hard to wish to help, to be capable of offering capable help, and not find a market for it, I thought as I plodded back across the night-dark yard. There were lights on in my father's quarters and in what had been my mother's. But no one was at the window, spying on unidentifiable flaunters of stupid rules.

I looked over my shoulder at the despicable internment camp and saw the guards on their rounds between the glowbasket standards. Was that where my soup and syrup would go? If that was its destination, my day had been profitable. With my spirits lifted, I continued back to the Hold.

Chapter VI

3.16.43

*C*ampen found me the next morning preparing to make more soup. "So this is where you are! Anella is looking for you."

"She's been looking for a Lady Nalka, and there is no one by that name in the Hold."

Campen snorted with disgust. "You know perfectly well she means you."

"Then she should summon me by name. I'll not go otherwise."

"In the meantime, she's making life very difficult for our sisters, and they miss our mother enough without having to put up with her carp-ings."

I was instantly repentant. In my own misery and guilt, I had forgotten that Lilla and Nia needed my presence and support.

"She must have new gowns, suitable to her position. Your needlework is the best."

"Kista was the best needlewoman among us," I told him angrily. "And Merin sewed the straight-est seam. But I'll go."

It was not a pleasant interview, and I knew that my behavior could be faulted on several counts. To add insult to injury, Anella was younger than I by several Turns, and keenly aware of that and of my greater height. But, knowing that I had deliberately disregarded her summonses, I took the tongue-lashing in silence, and took some con-solation in the fact that she had to crane her neck at an awkward angle to berate me. She looked like a wherry hen, strutting about in a heavy dressing gown far too ornate to suit her thin body and falling off her bottle-necked shoulders so that she had to jerk it frequently back into place. She lacked dignity, experience, sense, and humor.

"So how do you account for your absence these past two days? Where have you been? For if you've been sneaking off to meet some holder—"

At that accusation I decided I had had enough of her rantings. "I have been preparing restorative soups and cough syrups, and checking our medicinal supplies in case they should be needed." She flushed at my reminder of the present crisis. "The pharmacy has been my responsibility in this Hold."

"Why wasn't I told that was where you were? Your father—" She abruptly closed her lips.

"My father would not have known my especial duties. It was my mother's place to order such domestic affairs."

She gave me a searching glance, but I had kept my voice bland and chosen my words carefully.

"No one around here tells me anything I need to know," she complained. "If your name is not Nalka, what is it?"

"Nerilka."

"Close enough. Why did you not come at my bidding?" She grew angry again.

"I was not told."

"But they knew you were the one I wanted to see!"

"The entire Hold is still distracted by grief and anxiety."

She clamped her lips into a thin line, but what she wished to say was sparking out of her eyes, which were beginning once again to protrude with her attempts to control her agitations. She swished off to the window and stood looking out, twitching the gown back up her shoulders several times. Abruptly she whirled back.

"Your mother had everything so well organized in this Hold that I'm sure she had drapery stores and patterns. You may come with me to choose suitable lengths for my new wardrobe."

"Aunt Sira is in charge of Weaving."

"I don't need the Weaving Aunt. I need your sewing skills. You have those as well, do you not?" When I nodded, she went on. "Now where are the keys?" I pointed to the small chest on top of the press. With a cry of exasperation she leaped toward it, wrenching the drawer out in her haste to secure the keys to her new dignities. She had to hold the massive ring in both hands. "But which one? And which unlocks the jewelry safe? And the spice closet?"

"The stories are color-coded. The housekeeping keys are the smaller ones, room keys the larger. Hall keys larger still, and gold. All kitchen stores are green."

So I was forced to spend the rest of the morning taking my stepmother from story to story and as far down the sublevels as she insisted we go. I answered every question willingly and fully, but volunteered no information without seeming to withhold any. Afterward, I don't know if I was more disgusted with myself or with her general ignorance of Hold management. Had her mother not required her to do anything, and she the only daughter in the hold? I only hoped that my father would rue the day he let his infatuation overwhelm common sense. And the inconsistency of his complaint against my one suitor, Garben, who came from, no more or less, the same sort of family as Anella's. I also knew suddenly, and with complete certainty, that I would not be in Fort Hold to see his awakening to reality.

Anella required my presence to cut and start seaming several gowns for herself. She had some sense in her, for she said that Lilla and Nia could have tunics from the remnants of the three lengths. That ensured their cooperation and diligence on her clothes. I excused myself as soon as the work was well started, on the pretext that I must discharge my duties as pharmacist.

And so, in the Harper Hall, I learned for the first time of the blood serum injections that had been administered just the day before, and I heard, in a somewhat garbled fashion, of Master Capiam's recollection of this ancient method of giving a small dose of a disease to prevent a more disastrous illness. Healers had been given the first injections, as they would most need protection against the plague. Master Fortine had succumbed to it, received the treatment, and was suffering only minor discomfort. Soon, very soon, there would be enough of this liquid miracle to prevent any more healthy people from suffering the rigors of the plague. Pern was saved!

I took leave to doubt that enthusiastic report, but certainly the whole atmosphere of the Hall was charged with hope and relief. I immediately returned to the Hold, reprieved from the despair of more deaths among my loved ones. I rushed up to the sewing room to tell my sisters the good news. Anella was there, of course, supervising their stitches. She questioned me closely, making me repeat my news several times before she rushed off. Maybe she actually cared more for my father's health than for his Hold.

How it came to be, I do not know, but by evening, three healers arrived at the Hold and were shown immediately up to my father's quarters. I assume they inoculated him first. I'm certain that Anella was second, and then her babes. To my complete surprise, the immediate family was also injected, my younger sisters enduring the prick of the needlethorn without a whimper.

"There's enough left for fifteen more, Lady Nerilka. Whom would you suggest?" the healer journeyman asked me. "Desdra said you'd know." He had spoken quietly to me as I received the injection.

I told him to do all the Nursery adults, our three harpers, Felim and his chief assistant, Uncle Munchaun, and Sira, for she alone knew all the brocade patterns that were our especial Hold pride. And the chief bailiff, Barndy, and his son. With my father still immured in his rooms, Barndy was a key person and his son only slightly less so. Munchaun would take their part if that became necessary, and he was the only one who could shout Tolocamp down without reprisal.

3.17.43

I was required to spend most of the morning sewing in Anella's presence while she stood over my sisters and me, criticizing our stitches, making us pick out and do over—as often as not missing our poorer work—until I could stand it no more. Lilla, Nia, and Mara were more inclined to diligence, since they could anticipate, I hoped, to have new tunics for their labors.

Anella also had the poor taste to recount to us Tolocamp's injunctions to his bailiff and my brothers that there was to be no disposition of Fort Hold's stores to the indigent. All must be reserved for the needs of Fort Hold's dependents. This was a critical time, and Fort must stand firm, as an example to the rest of the continent. For instance, Anella relished reporting, Tolocamp was certain that the Healer and Harper would be applying to the Hold for substantial aid of food and medicine. He had received a formal request for an interview with Master Capiam and Master Tirone the next morning.

That, for me, was the final straw. I had now come to the end of patience, courtesy, and filial loyalty. I could no longer endure that woman's presence or remain a dependent of a man whose cowardice and parsimony made a disgrace of my Bloodline. I would no longer remain in a dishonored Hold.

On the grounds that I had a confectionary recipe that I wished to prepare for the evening meal, I excused myself. I went down to the kitchens, and on to the dispensary. There I distilled fellis in the largest kettle and brewed an equally large batch of the tussilago syrup. While these were simmering, I rifled the overstuffed shelves, taking a generous portion of every herb, root, stalk, leaf, blossom, and tuber that might possibly be of use to the Healer Hall. These I packaged, tying them securely and leaving them in a shadowy corner of the inner storeroom against the unlikely chance that Anella might inspect the facility. I decanted the fellis and tussilago into padded demijohns and added to these surreptitious stores a pack containing clothing necessities for myself. Then I made the sticky sweet for the evening meal, enough to surfeit Anella and her parents.

That evening I sought out Uncle Munchaun and gave him my mother's jewels to distribute to my sisters.

"Like that, eh?" He hefted the hide-wrapped packet of jewelry. "Did you not keep some by you?"

"A few pieces. I doubt jewelry will be required where I intend to go from here."

"Send me word when you can, Rill. I shall miss you."

"And I you, Uncle. You'll keep watch over my sisters?"

"Have I not always done so?"

"Better than most." I could not say more or weaken my resolution, so I fled down the steps from the second story.

3.18.43

    The next day, I had dutifully started yet another kettle of restorative soup in the small kitchen when I saw the Masterharper and the Masterhealer making their way across the Great Court for their interview with Tolocamp. I caught Sim's attention and told him to take two others and wait for me outside the dispensary. I had a task to be done.

I changed from my dress into garb suitable for what I hoped to be allowed to do, and stuffed a few last personal things in my belt pouch. I caught a glimpse of myself in the little mirror on my wall. It took me a moment: my hair had been my one vanity. I picked up the scissors and ruthlessly, before my resolution faltered, I cut off my long braids and stuffed them into the darkest corner of the press. No one would think to search my room for some time to come. My shorn hair suited my new role in life.

With a leather thong, I tied back what was left of my thick black hair. Then I left the room that had been my refuge since my eighteenth summer and made my way down the spiral stairs to my father's first-story apartment.

There was a convenient alcove on the inner wall just beyond the main door to his quarters. I had no sooner taken up my position when the drums announced the happy tidings that Orlith had laid a fine clutch of twenty-five eggs, including a queen egg. I'll bet there was considerable jubilation at Fort Weyr on that score. And it was certainly heartening news, though suddenly I could hear my father's mournful tones. Was he displeased with twenty-five and a queen? In ordinary times he would have called for wine to celebrate.

There was no one in the Hall, and at this hour in the morning most would be about their duties in or outside the Hold. I stepped close to the door and, by putting my ear to the wood, was able to hear most of what was said. Both Capiam and Tirone had good strong voices, and as they became more annoyed, their voices rose. It was my father who mumbled.

"Twenty-five with a queen egg is a superb clutch this late in a Pass," Capiam was saying.

"Moreta . . . mumble . . . Kadith . . . Sh'gall . . . so ill."

"That is not *our* business," I heard Master Tirone remark. "Not that the illness of the rider has any effect on the performance of the dragon. Anyway, Sh'gall is flying Fall at Nerat, so he's evidently fully recovered."

I had known that both Fort Weyrleaders had been ill and had recovered, for Jallora had been hastily dispatched from the Healer Hall when the Weyr healer had died. Why Sh'gall was flying at Nerat was beyond my source of information.

"I wish they would inform us of the status of each Weyr," my father said. "I worry so."

"The *Weyrs*"—Tirone spoke with emphasis — "have been discharging their traditional duties to their Holds!"

"Did *I* bring the illness to the Weyrs?" my father demanded, more loudly and quite petulantly, I thought. "Or the Holds? If the dragonriders were not too quick to fly here and there—"

"And Lords Holder not so eager to fill every nook and cranny of their—" Capiam was angry, too.

"This is *not* the time for recriminations!" Tirone interrupted them quickly. "You know as well as, if not better than, most people, Tolocamp, that seamen introduced that abomination onto the continent!" The Masterharper's voice dripped with disapproval. I hoped my father was fully

aware of it. "Let us resume the discussion interrupted by such good news. I have men seriously
ill in that camp of yours. There is not enough
vaccine to mitigate the disease, but they could at
least have the benefit of decent quarters and prac-
tical nursing."

So I had been correct in my assumption that
my father's parsimonious attitude extended to the
two Halls that Fort had traditionally supplied gen-
erously whenever approached.

"Healers are among them," my father coun-
tered in a sullen tone. "Or so you tell me!"

"Healers are not immune to the viral influence
and they cannot work without medicines," Capiam said urgently. "You have a great storehouse
of medicinal supplies—"

"Garnered and prepared by my lost Lady—"
How dare he speak in that maudlin fashion of my
mother!

"Lord Tolocamp," and I could hear the irrita-
tion in Master Capiam's voice, "we *need* those
supplies—"

"For Ruatha, eh?"

Surely my father didn't blame Ruatha for the
tragedy?

"Other holds besides Ruatha have needs!"
Capiam replied, as if Ruatha was indeed the very
last one on his list.

"Supplies are the responsibility of the individual holder. Not mine. I cannot further deplete

resources that might be needed by my own people."

"If the Weyrs," and Tirone's deep voice rang with feeling as he took up the argument, "stricken as they are, can extend *their* responsibilities in the magnificent way they have, beyond the areas beholden to them, then how can you refuse?"

I was stunned at my father's insensitive reply. "Very easily. By saying no. No one may pass the perimeter into the Hold from any outlying area. If they don't have the plague, they have other, equally infectious, diseases. I shall not risk more of my people. I shall make no further contributions from my stores."

Had my father not heard a single one of the messages, announcing the thousands of deaths in Keroon, Ista, Igen, Telgar, and Ruatha? My mother and four sisters were dead and quite likely the guards and the servants who had accompanied them, but they numbered only forty in all, not four hundred or four thousand or forty thousand.

"Then I withdraw my healers from your Hold." I nearly cheered Capiam's statement.

"But—but—you can't *do* that!"

"Indeed he can. *We* can," Master Tirone replied. I heard the scrape of his chair as he pushed it back from the table. I clapped my hands over my mouth lest I make any sound. "Craftsmen are under the jurisdiction of their Hall. You'd forgotten that, hadn't you?"

I had just enough time to get back into the shadows as the door was pulled roughly open and Capiam swung into the hall. The light from my father's windows showed me the anger on the Masterhealer's face. Master Tirone slammed the door shut.

"I'll call them out! Then I'll join you in the camp."

"I didn't think it would come to this!" Capiam was grim.

I inhaled, afraid for one moment that they might renege—this opposition was just what Tolocamp needed to bring him back to his lost senses.

"Tolocamp has presumed once too often on the generosity of the Halls! I hope this example reminds others of our prerogatives."

"Call our Craftspeople out, but don't come to the camp with me, Tirone. You must stay in the hall with your people, and guide mine!"

"My people"—Tirone gave a harsh laugh—"with very few exceptions, are languishing in that blighted camp of his. You are the one who must bide at the halls."

I knew then where I would go when I left this Hold, and I knew what I could do to expiate my father's intransigence.

"Master Capiam—" I stepped forward. "I have

the storeroom keys." I held up the duplicates my mother had given me on my sixteenth birthday.

"How did you?. . ." Tirone began, leaning forward to peer at my face. He didn't know who I was any more than Capiam did, but they knew I was one of the Fort Horde.

"Lord Tolocamp made plain his position when he received the request for medicines. I helped harvest and preserve them."

"Lady? . . ." Capiam waited for me to speak my name, but his voice was kind and his manner gentle.

"Nerilka," I said quickly, for I didn't expect so exalted a man to have known it. "I have the right to offer you the products of my own labor." Tirone was realizing that I had eavesdropped on their conversation, but I hardly cared. "There is just one condition." I let the keys swing from my fingers.

"If it is within my giving," Capiam replied tactfully.

"That I may leave this Hold in your company and work with the sick in that horrid camp. I've been vaccinated. *Lord* Tolocamp was expansive that day. Be that as it may, I will not stay in a Hold to be abused by a girl younger than myself. Tolocamp permitted her and her family to enter this hallowed Hold from the fire-heights yet he leaves healers and harpers to die out there!" I nearly added, "as he left my mother and sisters to die at Ruatha." Instead I pulled at Capiam's sleeve. "This way, quickly."

Tolocamp would recover from his shock at their ultimatum and start roaring for Barndy or one of my brothers.

"I'll remove our Craftspeople from this Hold on my way out," Tirone said. He turned and walked the other way.

"Young woman, you do realize that once you leave the Hold without your father's knowledge, particularly in his present frame of mind—"

"Master Capiam, I doubt he'll notice I'm gone." Maybe he was the one who had told Anella that my name was Nalka. "These steps are very steep," I warned, suddenly remembering that the Masterhealer wasn't used to the back ways. I flicked on a handglow.

Capiam stumbled once or twice as we spiraled down, and I heard him draw a sigh of relief as we turned into the larger corridor toward the storerooms. Sim was lounging on the bench with the other two.

"You are prompt, I see." I nodded reassurance at Sim, who hadn't expected to see the Master-healer down here. "Father appreciates prompt-ness." I included Master Capiam in that remark as I opened the door.

I went in first, flicking open the glowbaskets, and heard Capiam exclaim now that he recog-nized the room where he and my mother had often treated the Hold sick. I went into the main storeroom.

"Behold, Master Capiam, the produce of my labors since I was old enough to snip leaf and blossom or dig root and bulb. I won't say I have filled every shelf, but my sisters who have predeceased me would not deny me their portions. Would that all of these hoarded supplies were usable, but even herbs and roots lose their potency in time. Waste, that's the bulk of what you see, fattening tunnel snakes." I had heard the slither as the reptiles fled from the glowlights. "Carry-yokes are in the corner there, Sim." I raised my voice now, for my other remarks had been for the Masterhealer's ears so that he knew that what I gave him today did not seriously deplete those treasured stores Tolocamp must reserve for his own people. "You and the others, take up the bales." When I saw them start to load up, I turned to Master Capiam. "Master Capiam, if you do not mind—that's the fellis juice. I'll take this." I hefted the other demijohn by its girth strap and slung the pack over my shoulder. "I mixed fresh tussilago last night, Master Capiam. That's right, Sim. On your way now. We'll use the kitchen exit. Lord Tolocamp has been complaining again about the wear on the main hall carpets," I said quite mendaciously. "It's as well to comply with his instructions even if it does mean extra lengths for the rest of us."

Anne McCaffrey

I covered the glowbaskets and set down the demi-john to lock the storeroom, ignoring Capiam's expression. It didn't matter what he thought as long as I could leave the Hold without being seen.

"I would like to take more, but four drudges added to the noon parade to the perimeter are not going to be noticed by the guard." He spared a look at my clothing then. "No one will care in the least if one of the drudges continues on to the camp. Nor will anyone at the kitchen exit think it odd for the Masterhealer to leave with supplies." I had accustomed them to such traffic to the Hall. "Indeed, they would wonder if you left empty-handed."

I had finished locking up and now I dangled the keys before me. I couldn't just hang them on the door. "One never knows, does one?" I commented, stuffing them back into my belt pouch. "My stepmother has another set. She thinks it is the only one. But *my* mother thought the stillroom a very good occupation for me. This way, Master Capiam."

He followed me and I kept expecting any moment to hear an exhortation or good advice.

"Lady Nerilka, if you leave now—"

"I *am* leaving—"

"—and in this fashion, Lord Tolocamp—"

I stopped in my tracks and faced the man. It wouldn't do to be heard arguing with him as we crossed the kitchen. "—will miss neither me nor my dower." As I hefted the demijohn, I saw Sim exiting by the side door, and thought I had best be at his heels or he might falter. "I can be of real use in the internment camp for I know about mixing medicines and decocting and infusing herbs. I shall be doing something constructive that is needed rather than sitting comfortably in a corner somewhere." I did not add sewing straight seams to adorn my stepmother. "I know your craftsmen are overworked. Every hand is needed.

"Besides"—I touched the keys in my pouch— "I can slip back in whenever it's necessary. Don't look surprised. The drudges do it all the time. Why shouldn't I?" Especially when I am dressed as a drudge, I noted wryly.

I had to catch up to Sim and the others to maintain our cover; I also had to remember to move like a drudge. As I passed under the lintel of the kitchen door, I slumped my shoulders, lowered my head, canted my knees at each other for a more awkward gait, and pretended to be weighed down by my burdens, scuffing my feet in the dust.

Master Capiam was looking to our left, to the main forecourt and stairs where Master Tirone was moving down the ramp along with the healers who tended our elderlies, and the three harpers.

"He'll be watching them! Not us," I told Master

Capiam, for I, too, had caught sight of my father's figure in the open window. Maybe he'd catch his death of a cold. "Try to walk less proudly, Master Capiam. You are, for the moment, merely a drudge, burdened and reluctantly heading for the perimeter, terrified of coming down sick to die like everyone in the camp."

"Everyone in the camp is not dying."

"Of course not," I said hastily, hearing the anger in his voice. "But Lord Tolocamp thinks so. He has so informed us constantly. Ah, a belated attempt on his part to prevent the exodus!" I caught sight of the helmet tips over the balustrade. "Don't pause!" The Masterhealer had stopped briefly, and I didn't want anything to call attention to us. The departure of healers and harpers was a useful diversion. "You can walk as slowly as you want, that's in character, but don't stop."

I kept my head turned to the left, but then drudges were always attempting to ignore what they were supposed to be doing in favor of any activity that appeared more interesting. Seeing guards chasing after healers and harpers was very interesting. Especially guards who did not wish to follow their particular orders. I could just imagine Barndy's consternation. "Arrest the Masterharper, Lord Tolocamp? Now how could I do such a thing? The healers, too? Are they not

needed more in their own Hall right now than
here?"

There was a brief scuffle as Tirone barged
through the halfhearted attempt to thwart him.
I suppose words were exchanged between the
guards and the others, but no one truly interfered
with those departing, and Master Tirone led them
all down onto the road at a good pace.

Our path had already taken us across the roadway, and their steps would cover our footprints
in the dust. I continued my awkward pace and
wondered if my father even noticed the passing
of the drudges. Sim and the other two had
reached the perimeter, and Theng was looking
with some disgust at their burdens. He had come
hastily out of his little hut, but then he identified
the basket holding the noon meal of the guard
contingent and relaxed.

I began to worry about Master Capiam immured in the camp when he really ought to remain in his Hall, no matter what he had said to
Master Tirone.

"If you go past the perimeter, Master Capiam,
you will not be permitted back."

"If there is more than one way into the Hold,
is there only one past the perimeter?" he asked
me flippantly. "I'll see you later, Lady Nerilka."

I was relieved to think he was right. I was close
enough to the dip in the roadway to see the en-
campment, and the men and women, well back

of the guarded zone, waiting patiently for the food.

"Here now, Master Capiam." Theng came up, alarmed to see the resolution in the Masterhealer's stride. "You can't go in there without staying—"

"I don't want this medicine heaved about, Theng. Make sure they understand it's fragile."

I turned to one side, pretending to ease the weight of the demijohn. Theng knew me well enough to raise a commotion if he recognized me.

"I can do that much for you," Theng replied. He placed the demijohn to one side of the bales, then yelled down to the waiting men and women. "This is to be handled carefully, and preferably by a healer. Master Capiam says it's medicine."

I wanted to tell Capiam that I would see that the medicine was given to the appropriate people, but I dared not get too close to Theng, who was now making sure that Master Capiam went back where he belonged. I took the opportunity and walked quickly down the slope to the waiting people.

"Nah, then, Master Capiam," Theng was saying as I made good my escape, "you know I can't allow you close contact with any of your craftsmen."

I was immensely relieved that Theng intervened at that point. It was presumptuous of me, perhaps, but I felt that Master Capiam ought to remain where he was accessible to drum messages and councils with other Masters, particularly when he and the Masterharper had just pulled their Craftsmen from Fort Hold. As devoted a Craftsman as he was, it was not right that Master Capiam put himself at risk in this wretched camp. Perhaps now that the vaccine was being processed, the internment camp would be dispersed in only a matter of days. It would be a long time, however, before Hold, Hall, and Weyr could pick up the skein of routine and unravel the tangle in which the plague had left us.

I had a very selfish reason for being glad that Master Capiam had elected to stay above. I wished to change my identity as well as my Hold. One or two harpers or healers might recognize me from their attendance at the Hold, but they wouldn't be looking for Lady Nerilka here in the internment camp, surrounded by infection and vulnerable to discomfort as well as death.

Although she had not said so, Desdra undoubtedly had refused my offers of assistance because she knew that young ladies of Hold Blood did not engage in such activities on a public basis. She probably considered me a feckless, trivial person and perhaps I was: Some of my recent thoughts and decisions could have been considered petty. But I did not consider that I was sacrificing my high rank and position. I thought, rather, that I was putting myself in the way of being useful, instead of immured in a Hold, protected and unproductive, wasting my energy on trivia like sewing for my stepmother. Such a "suitable occupation" for a girl of my rank could so easily be undertaken by the least drudge from the linen rooms.

These thoughts fleeted through my head as I kept up the awkward gait I had assumed—ironic, as Hold girls were taught to take such tiny steps that they appeared to float across the floor. I had never quite mastered that skill. I followed the men and women who had brought the baskets to the perimeter. Now I could see that most of them wore harper knots. One man wore the colors of the River Hold, and another of the Sea Hold. Travelers trapped on their way to seek help from Tolocamp? The path turned off into the copse, where I could now see that rude shelters had been erected. We had been indeed fortunate that the weather had been so clement, for the third month was generally blustery, often blizzardy, and freezing cold. Each open fire in its ring of stones wore either spit or kettle iron. Was this where my restorative soups had gone? Then I realized that those huddled in blankets or hides about each fire had the gray complexions and lackluster expressions of convalescents.

One larger shelter, its sides made of an odd assortment of materials, was set to one edge of the copse, and from it issued a chorus of rasping coughs and groans that labeled it the main infirmary. It was toward this that the demijohn of fellis was being taken. Those carrying the baskets of food were beginning to distribute bread to those at the fires. Three women began to sort the vegetables and meat scraps into kettles. The silence was the worst of the scene.

I hastened to the infirmary and was met at the door by a tall, unshaven healer. "Fellis, herbs— what have you?" he asked eagerly.

"Tussilago. Lady Nerilka made it fresh last night."

He grimaced and took the demijohn from me. "It's heartening to know not everyone there agrees with the Lord Holder."

"He's a hypocritical coward."

The healer raised eyebrows in surprise. "Young woman, it is unwise to speak of your Lord Holder in that fashion, no matter what the provocation."

"He is not my Lord Holder," I replied, meeting his stare unflinchingly. "I have come to help. I have a firm grounding of the properties of herbs and their preparation. I . . . helped Lady Nerilka brew the tussilago. She taught me all I know, she and her lady mother now dead at Ruatha. I can nurse and I am not afraid of the plague. All I loved is dead now anyway."

He put a comforting hand on my shoulder. No one would dare such a familiarity toward the Lady

Nerilka, yet I did not find it offensive to be handled. It proved I was a human being.

"You are not alone in that." He paused for me to fill in my name. "All right, Rill, I'll take any volunteers right now. My best nurse just succumbed . . ." He nodded to a woman, still and white on a pallet of boughs. "There isn't all that much we can do except relieve the symptoms—" he affectionately patted the container of tussilago "—and hope there are no secondary infections. It is that which causes death, not the plague itself."

"There will soon be enough vaccine." I said it to cheer him, for patently he did not like to be so helpless in the face of this epidemic.

"Where did you hear that, Rill?" He had lowered his voice, and now held my upper arm in a painful grip. All handling is not reassuring.

"It is known. Yesterday the Bloods were inoculated against the disease. More of the serum is being made. You are nearby . . ."

The man shrugged in bitter acceptance of his situation. "Nearby, but scarcely a priority."

The woman struggled in the grip of the fever and flung herself out of her coverings. I went immediately to her side. And that began my first twenty-hour day as a nurse. There were three of us and Macabir, the journeyman healer, to tend the sixty stricken people in that rude infirmary. I never did know how many more the camp held, for the population shifted. Some had arrived on foot as well as by runner, hoping to claim Hold at Fort or assistance from the Halls or the Hold, and left when they realized that they were not permitted to reach their objective. I often wondered how many people actually had obeyed the full quarantine. But we are more populous here in the west than the eastern half of the continent. And the territory under Fort's jurisdiction suffered nowhere near the casualties that Ruatha did. We heard that only Master Capiam's early attendance at South Boll kept the disease from ravaging that province as well. There were those who said that Ratoshigan would have deserved the fate that was dropped on Ruatha and young Lord Alessan.

He was still alive, I learned. But he and his youngest sister were the only survivors of that Bloodline. His losses were more grievous than mine, then. Would his gains be as great?

Though harried, anxious, overworked, underfed, and certainly sleep-deprived, I had never been so happy. Happy? That is a very odd word to use in conjunction with my occupation in the camp, for that day and the next, we lost twelve of the sixty lying in the tent, and acquired fifteen in their places. But I was being useful for the first time in my life, and needed, and I was the amazed recipient of the mute gratitude of those I tended. For someone raised as I had been, the experience was a revelation in some rather personal and unpleasant ways as well, for I had never coped with the intimate bodily functions of either man or woman, and now had to attend both. I suppressed my initial revulsion and nausea, cropped my hair even shorter, rolled up my sleeves, and got on with the job. If this was part of it, then it would not be shirked.

I had the added assurance of knowing I was buffered against catching the disease that I nursed, so sometimes Macabir's praise of my courage on this count embarrassed me. Then a journeyman healer walked boldly into the camp bearing sufficient serum to inoculate everyone, and announced that the camp was being struck. The sick would be transported to the Harper Hall, where the apprentice barracks were being cleared to accommodate them. The transients also would find overnight shelter before being sped on their way in the morning. And if they'd be good enough to take along some supplies . . .

I volunteered, although Macabir repeated his wish for me to take formal training at the Hall. "You've a natural gift for the profession, Rill."

"I'm far too old to be an apprentice, Macabir."

"How old is old when you've a right knack with the sick? A Turn and you've done the initial training. Three, and there wouldn't be a healer who'd not be pleased to have you assist him."

"I'm free now to see more of this continent than one Hold, Macabir."

He sighed, scrubbing at his lined and weary face. "Well, keep it in mind if you find travel palls."

Chapter VII
3. 19. 43 – 3. 20. 43

I *left in the early evening light, with* a rough map to show me the way to three northern holds, quite close to the Ruathan border, where serum and other urgent medicinal supplies were needed. Macabir tried to persuade me to wait until the morning, but I reminded him that there was light enough with the full moon to travel those open roads, and the need was immediate. I wanted to take no chance that Desdra or someone from the Hold might recognize Lady Nerilka, disheveled and worn though she was.

I rode past Fort Hold, without so much as a glance to see if Tolocamp was at his window, past the cot ranks and the beastholds, and wondered if any one of the many people with whom I had spent my life up until two days ago saw me pass. Had anyone, indeed, with the exception of Anella and my sisters, missed me?

My folly was that I was more fatigued than I had suspected before the routine of nursing was stripped from me. I dozed half a dozen times in the saddle. Fortunately the runner was an honest beast, and once set on the track, continued for lack of other instruction. Reaching the first hold by midnight, I managed to inject the household before I collapsed. They let me sleep myself out, for which I berated the good lady when she fed me a huge breakfast at dawn, but she merely replied that the other holds knew I was coming and that was certainly better than wondering if they'd been totally forgotten.

So I rode on, arriving at the second hold by midmorning. They insisted that I stay for a meal, for I looked so tired and worn. They knew that there was no sickness at my final stop, and they were anxious for all the news I could give them. Until my arrival, they had been kept informed only by drum messages from my next stop, High Hill Hold, right on the border of Ruatha.

I finally admitted to myself that I was on my way to Ruatha. I had been unconsciously drawn toward that destination for many Turns, but had been thwarted so often by circumstance. Now, I reasoned to myself as I continued on the next leg of my journey, I had a skill to bring to that most tragic of Holds. Only dragonriders had been in to Ruatha Main Hold and rumors of the devastation were horrific. Well, I could nurse the sick, manage any area of Hold activity, and do what I could to expiate the guilt I still carried for the untimely deaths of my mother and sisters.

I was also beginning to realize that the plague had struck with a fine disregard for rank, health, age, and usefulness. It is true that the very young and the very old were more vulnerable, but the epidemic had claimed so many in the prime of life with so much living left to be done. If it suited me to clothe my action in the fine garb of sacrifice or expedience, as long as I performed the services required what matter the motives, hidden or open?

Arriving at High Hill Hold in the early afternoon, I was set immediately to work to stitch a long gash sustained by one of the holder's sons, despite my protestations that I was only a messenger. Their healer had gone down to Fort Hold when the news had been drummed out of Ruatha. Since I could tell them nothing of a man named Trelbin, they sadly realized that he, too, must be dead. Lady Gana said she was capable of dealing with minor cuts, but treating this wound was beyond her ability. Well, I had assisted at sufficient surgeries of this nature, so that I felt more confident in this instance than she obviously was.

Stitching a seam on fabric, which does not complain and cannot squirm, is quite a different matter from repairing ragged and uneven flesh. I had sufficient fellis and numbweed among the supplies I carried to ease the boy's discomfort and I sincerely hoped that my stitches held. Lady Gana announced herself impressed when I had finished.

Later I explained about the serum, then injected everyone except their high hold shepherds, who never came near enough to populated areas to catch an infection. Lady Gana was still not quite sure that the wind did not carry the disease, so she insisted that I tell her exactly how to cope with it. I know she did not believe me when I told her that death was not caused by the disease itself, but by secondary infections occurring in a patient already weakened. That is why I couldn't really admit that I was not a trained healer. I would undo all the good I had done. Whether I was trained or not, my information was accurate.

Bestrum and Gana then sadly related that a son and daughter accompanied by a servant had gone to the Ruathan Gather and they had had no word from them. They obviously hoped that I was bound for Ruatha.

Bestrum was laboriously sketching a map for me to follow when we were interrupted by excited shouts and cheers. Leaning out the windows we saw a blue dragon, curiously laden, settle to the ground. All of us rushed out to greet him.

"My name is M'barak, Arith's rider, of Fort Weyr. I come in search of more apprentice-blown glass bottles." The lad grinned engagingly as he pointed to the dragon's burdens. "Have you any you can spare Ruatha?"

However young, he had to be given the courtesies due a dragonrider, so over klah and some of Lady Gana's excellent wine cake, he told us that runnerbeasts also were dying of the plague, and needed to be inoculated. Bestrum and Gana took some pride in remarking that they had received their injections only that morning, and indicated me. I almost laughed as M'barak blinked, for I know he had assumed I was of this hold. Although I still wore coarse trousers and felt boots, Macabir had given me healer tunic and surcoat against the rigors of travel. I didn't look like a proper healer and I at least knew it, if the kind holders did not.

"Were you just going back to the Healer Hall now?" M'barak began. "Because if you happened to be handy with runnerbeasts, you'd be of tremendous use right now at Ruatha. I can take you—" his eyes twinkled with mischievous delight "—and save you a long and tedious journey. Tuero could drum the Hall to tell 'em where you are. It's just getting people up to Ruatha right now, people who've been injected and aren't afraid of the plague. You're not afraid, are you?"

I only shook my head, a bit shocked at the way my pulses had leaped and my heart skipped at this unexpected invitation to go where I desperately wanted to be. During Suriana's lifetime, Ruatha had been the lodestone for my only chance of some happiness and freedom. I had freed myself of Fort Hold's Blood yoke and was now equally free to go to Ruatha, especially now that I had been given what was tantamount to an invitation. It would be a Ruatha sadly changed from the Hold Suriana had described, but I would be of more use there now, especially going as Rill, not as Lady Nerilka. It was employment and purpose I sought, wasn't it?

"If it's someone good with runners you need, I've two men here spending their waking hours carving scrimshaw for lack of something to do till spring comes in earnest," Bestrum said expansively. "Rill jabbed 'em with the rest of us this morning, so they've no call to fear going to Ruatha."

So it was arranged. As the two beasthandlers, brothers sharing the same phlegmatic temperament and solid builds, collected their necessaries, Gana kindly fetched out a heavy cloak against the biting cold of *between*. She bustled about with her drudges, organizing provisions for three more mouths as well as collecting three great apprentice-blown glass jars, which M'barak and I had to arrange so as not to crack together on Arith.

This was by no means my first contact with a dragon, but certainly it was the most extended and personal. Dragons have a warm, very smooth soft hide, which leaves a spicy smell on your hands. Arith rumbled a lot, though M'barak assured me that it didn't mean he was annoyed with his unusual burden. We padded the great glass bottles; Fort had more than its share of these apprentice efforts, although I cannot remember what Mother did with them.

I made a final check on the boy's wound, but it looked unchanged and he was fast asleep, a smile on his face from the fellis. Then I took my farewell of Bestrum and Gana, who, though I had known them only a few hours, were profuse in their good wishes. I told them that I would ask about their children and the servant, and send back word. Gana knew there was slight hope, but the offer gave her comfort.

When Bestrum gave me a heave to the dragon's back, I thumped into place behind M'barak's slight but straight body and hoped I didn't hurt Arith. The two brothers got aboard with less fuss, and it was comforting to know that there were two behind me to fall off before I would be in danger.

Arith executed a little run before he jumped skyward, then his fragile-looking, transparent wings took the first mighty sweep downward. It was the most exhilarating experience I had ever had, and I envied dragonriders anew as Arith's strong wings carried us further aloft. I needed the cloak as well as the buffer of warm bodies in front and behind me.

M'barak must have known how I was feeling, for he turned his head and gave me a wide pleased grin. "Hold on now, Rill, we're going *between*," he yelled. At least, that's what I thought he must have said as the wind tore his voice away.

If flying dragonback is exhilarating, going *between* is the essence of terror. Blackness, nothingness, a cold so intense my extremities ached, and only the knowledge that riders and dragons experienced the same thing daily with no ill effect kept me from screaming in fear. Just as I was sure I would suffocate, we were sunstruck again as Arith brought us by that unique draconic instinct to our destination. Then I had far more to concern me than that fleeting passage through black *between*.

I had never been to Ruatha Hold, but Suriana had sent me innumerable sketches of the establishment and had described its amenities time and again. The great Hold, carved from the living

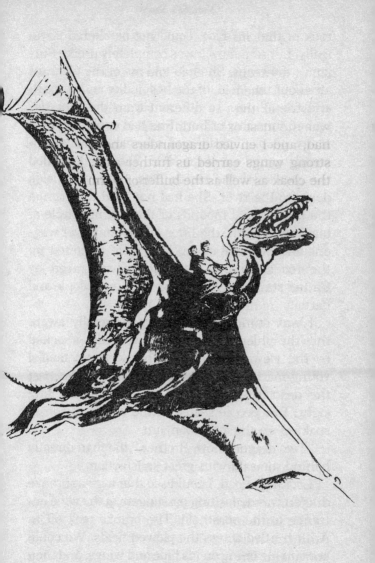

rock of the cliff face, could not be altered phys-
ically, but somehow it was completely unlike Suriana's drawings. She had told me of the pleasant
air about the Hold, of the hospitality and warmth
and friendliness so different from the cool, detached formality of Fort. She had explained how
many people, family and otherwise, were constantly in and out of the Hold. She had described
the meadows, the racing flats, the lovely fields
down to the river. She had not lived to describe
the huge burial mounds or the charnel circle of
blackened earth, the litter of broken travel wag-
ons and personal effects that were scattered up
the roadstead that had once been graced by
Gather stalls, bright with banners and people and
barter.

I was stunned, and only peripherally aware
that the phlegmatic brothers were also shocked
by the view. Mercifully, M'barak was a tactful
young man and said nothing as Arith glided past
the desolate Hold. I did see one encouraging
sight: five people seated in the court, obviously
soaking up the afternoon sun.

"Two dragons now, Brother," the man directly
behind me said with great satisfaction.

Looking ahead, I could see that a great bronze
dragon was depositing passengers at the wide entrance to the beasthold. The bronze took off as
Arith hurtled across the plowed fields. We could
see sun gleaming on his hide and wings, and then

he just disappeared. Arith settled down in exactly the same spot the bronze had occupied.

"Moreta," M'barak called, gesturing eagerly. The tall woman with short, curly blond hair turned back to him. The Fort Weyrwoman was the last person I expected to encounter at Ruatha.

I shall always remember that I had that opportunity to see Moreta again and at that particular moment in her life, when her face was tinged with sun and an inner serenity that I was not to understand until much later. She had, of course, been at Fort Hold in her capacity of Weyrwoman since she had assumed that responsibility on Leri's retirement. But these were infrequent visits —on state occasions—so although I had been in the same Hall with her, we had never actually spoken together. I had had the impression that she was shy or reticent, but then Tolocamp did so much talking in that ponderous way of his that I doubt she'd have had a chance to speak.

"Hurry up!" M'barak's voice hauled me away from my impressions of that moment. "I need help with these silly bottles and I've people here who say they can handle runners. And we've got to hurry because I have to prepare for the Fall. F'neldril will skin me if I'm late!"

Two other men and a slim, dark-haired girl moved out of the shadows to help. I knew Alessan on the instant and supposed the girl must be his surviving sister, Oklina. The other man wore

Harper blue. The brothers dismounted quickly, and M'barak and I handed down first the provisions and then the great bottles, none of which had suffered any travel damage.

"If you'll slip down, Moreta can mount," M'barak suggested, with a grin of apology for his haste.

So, for the first time, I traded places with Moreta. I would have liked to have sustained the contact then, for she had a manner about her that made one want to get to know her better. She appeared considerably less aloof than she had seemed in the Hold. As Arith began his preparatory little run, Moreta did look back over her shoulder. But it couldn't have been at me.

I turned and saw that Alessan had shaded his eyes to watch until the dragon went *between*. Then he smiled, his welcome taking me in along with the two brothers, and held out his hand in the friendliest way. "You've come to help us with the runners? Was M'barak frank about what is needed in ruined Ruatha?"

At first I thought he sounded bitter, but came to understand that he did not hide from the grim realities of his situation. He ever had a wry sense of humor, but Suriana, preparing me for my long-expected visit to Ruatha, had warned me of that. What would she think of her foster sister coming here like this?

"Bestrum sent us, Lord Alessan, with his condolences and greetings," said the more grizzled of the two men. "I'm Pol; my brother's Sal. We like runners better nor other beasts."

Alessan turned his smiling light-green eyes to me, and all that Suriana had told me about him rattled through my head. But the sketches that she had also sent did not do him justice, or else he had changed dramatically from that young and rather reckless-looking man. There was now considerably more character about the eyes and mouth, and an ineffable sadness, despite the smile of his greeting—a sadness that would fade, but never leave. He was thin, had been fever-gaunt; the broad bones of his shoulders pushed through his tunic and his hands were rough, calloused, cracked, and pricked, more like a common drudge's than a Lord Holder's.

"I'm Rill," I said, to bring myself back to the present and to guard against unexpected queries. "I have always managed runners. I've some experience in healing and concocting all kinds of medicines from herbs, roots, and tubers. And I've brought some supplies with me."

"Would you have anything for the racking cough?" the girl asked, her huge dark eyes shining. Such a shining could scarcely be for me or for the provision of cough syrup, but I did not know until much later how these people had spent the unusual hour that had just ended moments before we arrived.

"Yes, I do have," I said, hefting my saddlebags packed with the bottles of tussilago.

"Holder Bestrum wanted to know if his son and daughter live," Pol asked bluntly, shifting uncomfortably from foot to foot while his brother looked anywhere but at Lord Alessan.

"I'll look at the records," the harper said gently, but we had all noticed the shuddering expression that dampened the smile in Alessan's eyes. And Oklina had given a little gasp. "I'm Tuero," the harper went on, smiling to reassure us all. "Alessan, what's the order of business now?"

And so Tuero deftly turned our thoughts to the future, away from the sorrowful past. Shortly we had no time for anything, past or future. The present consumed us.

Alessan quickly explained what had to be done. First, the few patients still remaining in the Main Hall infirmary had to be moved to quarters on the second level of the Hold. Then the Hall must be scrubbed thoroughly with redwort solution. He looked beyond me, from whom he could expect assistance at such a task, to Pol and Sal.

"We must make sufficient serum to inoculate runnerbeasts." He turned and gestured toward the pasture. "We will take blood from those that survived the plague."

Pol stopped mid-nod and glanced at Sal. I must admit that I was stunned by the look of the runnerbeasts. Many were weedy, with light bones and high haunches, rather thin-necked and far too gaunt to bear any resemblance to the sturdily conformed, rugged, firm-fleshed beasts that had been the pride of Ruatha Hold. Some were no more than great walking bone racks.

Alessan noticed our consternation. "Most of the beasts that my father bred died of the plague." His tone was matter-of-fact and we took our cue from it. "Those that I had bred for speed over short distances turned out to be resilient and came through, as did some of the crossbreds that our guests had brought."

"Oh, the pity of it, the pity of it," Pol murmured, shaking his grizzled head. His brother did the same.

"Oh, I shall breed fine strong beasts again. Would you know my handler, Dag?" Alessan asked the brothers. They both brightened and nodded with more enthusiasm. "He'd some of the mares in foal and a young stallion up in the hill meadows. They survived, so I've some of the old basic stock to breed from."

"Good to hear, lord, good to hear." Sal's words were directed more to the runners than to Alessan.

"But—" Alessan grinned apologetically to the two men "—before we can start collecting blood for the serum, we have to have a clean and totally uncontaminated place in which to work."

Pol began rolling up his sleeve. "There isn't much my brother and I wouldn't do to help you, lord. We've scrubbed before, we can scrub again."

"Good then," Alessan said with a grin. "Because if we don't do it right the first time, journeywoman Desdra will make us do it all over again until we have! She'll be here tomorrow to check on our labors."

When we reached the courtyard before the Hold door, Tuero, a man named to me as Deefer, five fosterlings, and four of the convalescent farm holders were constructing a strange device from cart wheels.

"We'll have several of these centrifuges with which to separate the miracle serum from the blood," Alessan told us. The brothers nodded as if they knew exactly what he was talking about, though some confusion and surprise showed on Sal's face.

Oklina met us in the Hall, leading out the procession of drudges with their buckets of hot water, cleaning rags, and brooms. She carried containers which I recognized as those generally used to store the strong cleaning fluid. We all rolled up our sleeves and I noticed that Alessan's hands were red already, though there was only a fainter tinge of red on his upper arms. Then we all set to scrubbing.

We scrubbed until the glowbaskets were lit,

scrubbed even as we munched with meatrolls in one hand and tried to ignore the faint taste of astringency that the overpowering aroma of redwort invariably gave to anything in its vicinity. We scrubbed until the first sets of glowbaskets had to be replaced.

Alessan had to shake me several times before I left off the scrubbing motion and realized that the others had quit this labor. "You're all but asleep and still scrubbing, Rill," he said, but he spoke with such a kind sort of raillery that I gave him a rueful grin.

I had barely enough energy to follow Oklina up the stairs to the first-story inner room that she assigned me. I remembered that I bade her goodnight as I closed the door. I knew I should plan a few words to say to Desdra on her arrival the next day, so that she would not expose me as Tolocamp's mutinous daughter, but the moment I fell across the bed, I fell asleep.

Chapter VIII

3. 21. 43—3. 22. 43

I woke, startled, as people do at finding themselves in a strange place, and had to reassure myself that I was not back in my room at Fort Hold. It was silence that I heard so palpably, a silence that confused me more than did the slightly strange surroundings. Then I isolated the difference—no drums at all. I rose and dressed, and began my first full day at Ruatha.

I was in the Hall, drinking klah and eating a quick breakfast of porridge when Desdra arrived on Arith. We all went out at the commotion for the little dragon was once again draped with many bottles, the large apprentice size and the smaller ones for the all important serum.

I had no chance to speak with Desdra, for Alessan singled me out with the two brothers and took us off to the field to begin the next step in making the serum.

Either the animals were apathetic from their recent illness or they had been well-handled, so we were each able to lead in two at a time. A second and third trip filled all the stalls in the beasthold, then Alessan demonstrated how to draw blood from the neck vein. All the creatures kindly submitted to this bloodletting. Sal and I began to work as a team, and when I saw that he had little stomach for inserting the needle-thorn, I took over that job as he held each runner's head.

It was full noon before we had finished with the twenty-four beasts. After each drawing, the blood was decanted into the great apprentice jars, then transported to the Hall and secured onto the cartwheel centrifuges. Though I was not the only one dubious about the device, much less the process, Desdra's attitude towards the manufacture was so reassuringly calm that we didn't question anything. As soon as she had checked the fastenings, she motioned the crews of men to begin spinning the wheels. The men changed places at the flywheels frequently, always keeping the speed of the whirling at the same pace. I thought briefly what a mess one loose jar could make of the Hall, and all our cleaning to be done again, and then decided that such ruminations were unsuited to the general air of hope and industry in Ruatha.

Oklina passed among us then, with a hearty soup and warm bread rolls. When Desdra finally joined us, many of us crammed at one long trestle table and others leaning against the walls, she explained the urgency of our monumental task. Only a mass and instantaneous inoculation of threatened runners would prevent the plague from recurring. Everyone in Ruatha Hold would have some part in this enterprise, for the plague must not be permitted to have a second chance at decimating the continent. The news created a hushed silence.

While awaiting the results of the first batch, Pol, Sal, and I went back to the beasthold to see how our patients did. Dag was already mixing them a hearty meal of warmed bran with a fortified wine and some herbs, which the old handler said would strengthen the new blood. Then we groomed them well, taking the mud and burrs from their tails and manes.

Despite his splinted right leg, Dag worked right along with us. What he couldn't do for himself was accomplished by his grandson, a rascally, impudent, possessive lad named Fergal. He seemed suspicious of everyone, especially of Alessan when the lord came to see how the beasts had stood up to the bloodletting. The only person whose bidding Fergal would ever do without quibble was Oklina. Every other order he contested with questions that were sheer impudence. Dag, he adored. Obviously he thought the bandy-legged little runner handler could do no wrong. But, for all his insolence, Fergal was patently dedicated to the beasts. A very pregnant mare took most of his caring; swollen though she was in the last days of gestation, she had a way of cocking her head, ears pricking forward and whuffling at Fergal in a manner I thought most ingratiating.

"The first batch should be done soon," Alessan announced suddenly.

I was amused that, of the group working with the beasts, Fergal and I were the only ones eager to see the result. Pol and Sal ensconced themselves on bales for a comfortable chat with Dag, politely declining the invitation to see the finished serum.

What startled me was the odd straw-yellow fluid that was the product of this centrifugal process. By the time we got to the Hall, Desdra was already drawing it from one jar, explaining how this should be done without stirring up the darker residue. Under her direction, we tentatively began to imitate her, drawing the clear fluid from the jar, placing it in the glass bottles, using a clean needlethorn with each insertion to reduce the possibility of contamination. Ruthlessly, Desdra employed everyone at the Hall at this task, even three of the strongest convalescents, constantly moving among us to oversee the task.

"We should have more bottles this afternoon," Tuero told us. He meant to be cheerful but was rewarded by groans from all the workforce. "M'barak said he'd pass the word of our need during Fall."

"How much of this junk do we gotta have?" Fergal asked. He glanced out toward the fields where his beloved runners grazed.

"Enough to inoculate the mares and foals of the remaining herds in Keroon, Telgar, Ruatha, Fort, Boll, Igen, and Ista," Alessan said. I stifled a groan at the quantities that would be required.

"Ista doesn't breed runners. It's an island," Fergal said belligerently.

"It suffered the plague, man and beast," Tuero said when Alessan did not reply. "Keroon and Telgar are also producing this serum, so Ruatha doesn't have to do it all."

"Ruatha has that much, at least, to give Pern," Alessan added, as if no other comments had been made. "We will insure that the best possible serum comes from our beasts. Let us return to our tasks."

And so we persevered. Those who had not fully

114

recovered were put to sitting at sinks to scrub glassware or securely stopper the serum bottles and insert them in reed holders. The youngest became messengers or, in pairs, carefully carried crates of serum down to the cool rooms.

My job was bleeding runners. It was almost a relief to leave the pervading stench of redwort to bring my patient-victim back to the field and collect another one. At least I had some fresh air. Dag had started marking the bled ones with paint so we wouldn't inadvertently get two lots from the same beast. None of them were strong enough for that. My frequent walks also gave me a chance to observe ruined Ruatha, as Alessan called it. I could see that only a little time and effort would be required to put a lot of the ruin to rights, and I worked out the strategy going to and fro, planning all that I would do if I had the right to meddle in Ruathan affairs. A harmless enough pastime, to be sure.

The drums had begun midmorning, telling us what quantities were needed and which dragonriders would collect what amounts. Alessan explained that the quantities had to be listed accurately, but he really couldn't spare Tuero to listen to drum codes.

"Then have Rill do it," Desdra said bluntly.

"Can you understand drum messages, Rill?" Alessan asked, somewhat surprised. I had been taken so unaware that I couldn't answer. I had even begun to think that Desdra had not recognized Tolocamp's daughter in grimy, sweaty, short-haired Rill.

"And probably the codes as well, isn't that right, Rill?" Desdra was quite ruthless, but at least she did not explain to anyone how she knew so much about my unmentioned skills. "She can fill serum bottles between messages. She needs a bit of sit-down time. She's been going full pelt for some days now."

I took that to mean that Desdra approved of my labors here and at the internment camp and was permitting me my whimsy. Fortunately, not even Alessan questioned how a drudge who had risen to volunteer healer understood such arcane matters. But I was indeed grateful for the chance to sit down. How Alessan kept up his level of energy, I do not know. I could see why Suriana had admired as well as adored him. He deserved respect, and he had mine for new reasons at every turn. I could also perceive that he was driven. Somehow, despite all the brutal odds against him, Alessan was going to restore Ruatha Hold, repeople its vacant holds, restock its empty fields. I wanted to stay on here, and help him.

I was also discovering that once back in a formal Hall, I automatically assumed familiar responsibilities, such as ordering drudges to tasks or explaining how to do a job more efficiently. Fortunately, no one questioned my right to do so when it was all in the best interest of the work at hand.

Despite a deceptively frail appearance, Oklina worked as hard as her brother, but the sheer press of her obligations appalled me, who had always had sisters to ease burdens. Whenever I could, I lent her a hand. She wasn't a pretty girl, which the uncharitable might say was one reason I related to her so easily, for the dark complexion and strong features that became a man suited her no better than my family resemblance suited me. But she was an exceptionally graceful young woman, with a charming smile and great, dark, expressive eyes in which lurked a sort of secret bemusement. I often caught her gazing toward the northwest and wondered if she had fallen in love with some young man. She would make an excellent holder's wife, young though she was, and I devoutly hoped that Alessan would not require her to remain at Ruatha, but would settle her with a kind and generous man. Ruatha might be poverty-stricken now, but the prestige of the Bloodline was still undisputed. Nor would this altruistic labor on the serum, so willingly undertaken by Alessan and Oklina, reduce them in the estimation of their peers.

And so we worked on, turning from one urgent and necessary task to another, ladling a quick cup of soup from the pot simmering on the main hearth, or chewing from a hunk of fresh bread

in a free hand and a spare moment. From somewhere, fresh fruit had appeared—one of the dragonriders was dropping off supplies. Why ripe
melon slices would cause Oklina's eyes to tear, I
could not then fathom. I doubted that she was so
moved by the thoughtfulness behind the gift.
Then I noticed that Alessan regarded the fruit
with a soft smile of reminiscence, but he was off
to work again so quickly, bread in one hand, the
melon slice in the other, that I could have been
wrong. Then another message came in, and I had
to listen to record the message accurately.

Time had lost all order in the press of work. On
my third day at Ruatha, all but a few of us had
gone outside to eat a delayed and well-deserved
evening meal when suddenly Alessan, Desdra,
and Tuero, consulting the maps, lists, and charts,
gave out whoops of exultation.

"We've done it, my loyal crew!" Alessan
shouted. "We've got enough! And enough over
the requirement to take care of any spillage and
breakage in dispatching. It's wine all round!
Oklina, take Rill and get four flasks from my private store."

He tossed her a long slim key, which she
caught deftly in midair. She grabbed my hand
and, laughing with delight, hauled me to the
kitchen and then on down to the stores, beyond
the cold room.

"He is really pleased, Rill. He rarely parts with bottles of his own store." She giggled again. "He guards them for a special purpose." Then her charming little face saddened. "And I hope he will again," she added cryptically. "He must soon in any case. Here we are."

When she had unlocked the narrow door and showed me the racked flasks and wineskins, I gasped in astonishment. Even in the dim light from the glowbasket down the corridor, I could see the distinctive Benden flask. Quickly I dusted off a label.

"It *is* Benden white," I cried.

"You've had Benden white wine?"

"No, of course not." Tolocamp would not have approved of his daughters drinking rare vintages; the foxy Tillek pressings were good enough for us. "But I've heard about it." I managed to giggle. "Is it really as good as they say?"

"You can judge for yourself, Rill."

She locked the door again, then relieved me of half the burden.

"Did you finish your training at the Healer Hall, Rill?"

"No, no." Somehow I could not lie to Oklina even if it meant demeaning myself in her eyes. "I volunteered to help nurse, as I wasn't needed any longer in my own Hold."

"Oh, did your husband die of the plague?"

"I have none."

"Well, Alessan will see to that. That is, of course, if you wish to stay on in Ruatha. You've been such a help, Rill, and you seem to understand a great deal about Hold management. I mean, we shall have to start all over again, so many of our people died. There are many holds empty, and while Alessan is going to approach the holdless in hopes that some are suitable, I'd rather have a few people about us whom we already know and trust. Oh, Rill, I'm putting this so badly. But Alessan asked me to sound you out about staying on here at Ruatha. He has great respect for you. You have been such a help. Tuero—" Oklina giggled again "—plans to stay, no matter how he and Alessan go on about the salary and perks."

That discussion had been running between harper and Lord Holder whenever they passed each other or worked on a common chore. Tuero had come to the Gather with other harpers to assist the Hold's regular harper, another victim, as were Tuero's companions. I couldn't imagine Ruatha Hold without Alessan and Tuero bickering in the most amiable fashion.

When we returned to the Main Hall, the men had stacked some of the cartwheels and the large jars back against the wall. Alessan and Tuero were clearing space on the trestle table, where we had been consuming our hasty meals. Dag and Fergal came up from the kitchen with the stew; Deefer brought plates and cutlery; Desdra had an armful of bread loaves and a huge wooden bowl full of fruit and cheeses, including the one forwarded by Lady Gana. I wouldn't have thought that that would have lasted past my bringing it here. Follen arrived with the cups and the cork pull.

Outside I could hear the subdued revelry of the others who had now been released from their unremitting labors of the past two days.

So it was only the eight of Alessan's loyal crew, an odd assortment to sit down at any table for any meal, but the knowledge of an almost impossible task timely completed made companions of us all, even Fergal. He refused a cup of wine with an insolence that I'm certain Alessan excused only because the boy had worked so hard. I'd wager that Fergal was as knowledgeable about such restricted treats as anyone else here. Fergal's sort is born knowing. In spite of his impudence and suspicious nature, I did like the boy.

That dinner was a very happy event for me. Alessan had taken the seat next to me, and I found his proximity strangely agitating. I tried to avoid touching him, but we were rather crowded on the benches, companionably so for everyone else. Since he was close to me, his arm resting on the table touched mine, occasionally his thigh brushed mine, and he grinned at me when Tuero said something particularly amusing. My heart

raced, and I knew that my answering laugh was a little high and foolish. I was tired, I expect, over-reacting to the success we were celebrating, and very much unused to the fine white Benden wine.

Then Alessan leaned against me deliberately, touching my forearm with his fingertips. My skin tingled.

"What's your opinion of the Benden, Rill?"

"It's made me giddy," I replied quickly so that if he noticed my unusual behavior, he would know the reason, even though I wished to do nothing to lower myself in his good opinion.

"We all need to relax tonight. We all deserve it."

"You more than anyone else, Alessan."

He shrugged and looked down at his cup, his fingers idly twisting it around by the stem. "I do what I must," he said, speaking in a low voice. The others were involved in an argument.

"For Ruatha," I murmured.

He looked at me, mildly surprised at my re-joinder, his strange green-flecked eyes for once candid. "That's perceptive of you, Rill. Have I been such a hard taskmaster?"

"Not for Ruatha's sake."

"This—" he waved his hand at the cartwheels and empty jars "—has not been for Ruatha's sake."

"Oh, but it has. You said so yourself. Ruatha can do this much for Pern."

He gave a slightly embarrassed laugh. But his smile was kind, and I think he was pleased.

"Ruatha will be herself again! I know it!" It was safer to talk about Ruatha's future.

There was an odd expression in his eyes. "Then Oklina spoke to you? You'll consider staying on with us?"

"I would like to very much. The plague left me holdless."

His warm strong hand closed on mine, squeezing lightly in gratitude. "And do you have any special requirements, Rill, to cement our relationship?" There was a real gleam in his eye now as he tilted his head toward Tuero.

His question had come up so unexpectedly that I'd had no time to think about anything beyond the fact that my wish to remain in Ruatha had been granted. I stammered a bit, and then Alessan once again gripped my arm.

"Think about it, Rill, and tell me later. You'll find that I hold fair with my people."

"I'd be surprised to find aught else."

He grinned at my vehemence, poured more wine into my cup and his, and so we sealed the agreement in the traditional manner, though I had trouble swallowing past the lump of joy in my throat. Companionably, we finished bread and cheese, listening to the other conversations at the table and to the music outside.

"I wasn't so taken with that Master Balfor, Lord Alessan," Dag was saying, his eyes on the wine in his cup. He was speaking of the man presently designated to become Beastmaster at Keroon.

"He's not confirmed in the honor," Alessan said. I could see that he didn't wish to argue the matter right now, especially not in front of Fergal, who was always listening to matters he ought not hear.

"I'd worry who else might have the rank, for Master Balfor certainly hasn't the experience."

"He has done all that Master Capiam asked," Tuero said with an eye on Desdra.

"Ah, it's sad to realize how many good men and women have died." Dag lifted his cup in a silent toast, which we all drank. "And sadder to think of the fine bloodlines just wiped out. When I think of the races Squealer will walk away with and no competition to stretch him in a challenge. You say Runel died?" Dag went on. "Did all his bloodline go?"

"The oldest son and his family are safe in the hold."

"Ah, well, he's the right one for it. I'll just have a look at that brown mare. She could foal tonight. Come along, Fergal." Dag picked up his splinted leg and hauled it over the bench. For just a moment, Fergal looked rebellious.

"I'll come with you, if I may," I said, handing Dag the crutches. "A birth is a happy moment." I needed some clean night air to fill my lungs, and clear my head of all that good Benden wine. And I also needed to be away from Alessan's stimulating presence.

My heart was very full and beating erratically. I did not wish to embarrass Alessan with an overflow of gratitude, or any outpouring declaration of loyalty, though I felt both emotions intensely. By a freak of chance I had achieved a miracle: I had been invited to *stay* at Ruatha Hold. Forget that the rationale was prosaic; merely that I was useful, they trusted me, and Ruatha had to rebuild itself. I tried not to let my mind refine upon anything that Oklina had said, much less what Alessan had not. To be able to live at Ruatha was enough. I would be in his company, in the very place that had figured so often in my daydreams, that had been the focus of all happiness. Ruatha could once again be a happy place, and I would have the totally unexpected opportunity to achieve that.

Fergal was with us in a moment. He would not allow me to monopolize his grandfather's company.

The night was clear, the air was fresh, and I could feel spring ascending from the warmer climes. We exchanged nods and smiles with the people sitting before the spit fire and along the cot line. I carried the glowbasket to light our path, though all three of us knew each flag, pebble, and dip to the beasthold by now. Fergal ran on ahead.

"If she hasn't foaled by midnight, she's not likely to," Dag announced. "We need another colt."

"Who's the foal's sire?"

"One of old Lord Leef's burthen stallions, so it's a colt we need to bring the line back. You're staying on with us, are you, Rill?" Dag was generally blunt.

I nodded, unable to answer, the joy and relief at my good fortune too precious to talk about. Dag gave a curt nod of his shaggy head.

"We have need of folk like yourself. Any more where you come from?" He gave me a sly sideways glance.

"Not that I know of," I replied amiably, hoping to still his curiosity. We hadn't had much time for personal conversations these past two-and-a-half days. Now I saw that I would have to develop an appropriate previous history.

"Not every woman can turn her hand to most chores in Hold and beasthold. Were you in a fair-sized place before the plague?"

"Yes, and it saddens me to think of those I lost." Maybe that prevarication would suffice.

Some ethic in me refused to tell untruths. I sighed. One day the truth surely would come out, but by then I hoped to be so well established at Ruatha that I would be forgiven origin as well as defection.

Fortunately we had arrived at the beasthold. Pol and Sal were there, sitting on bales across from the mare, maintaining a discreet watch. They were soaping a leather harness from the pile of tack collected from Gather detritus as worth saving. Pol handed Fergal a breastplate, green with mold. The boy glanced first at Dag, who nodded, and then grimaced at Pol, but he sat himself down and took up a cloth. Dag and I found bales to sit on and straps to clean.

"Bestrum's second son's looking for cropland," Pol said out of the contented silence.

"Is he?" Dag asked.

"Strong lad, good worker, got a girl in mind from the next Hold."

"Think Bestrum will mind after losing the others here?"

"Likes Alessan. Boy'd do better here and Bestrum knows it. Fair man, Bestrum."

"For sending you and Sal, yes, he is." Dag kept nodding in approval. Then he looked up at Pol, eyes narrowed in speculation. "How long can he spare you? I've got all those mares to put to our stallions and this broken leg . . ."

"You said I'd be helping you, Dag," Fergal complained, glaring at Pol, who ignored him.

"So you will, lad, but there's more than two of us can handle."

"Spring comes later in the mountains," Pol said.

"We be-n't needed a while yet," Sal added.

"Shall I ask Holder Bestrum when I write Lady Gana about her children?" I asked.

"That would be kind of you."

Tuero had established that Lady Gana's daughter had died in the first wave of deaths, nursed by the old servant, who also succumbed. Both were buried in the first of the stark mounds. The son had worked hard helping Norman, the field manager of the racing flats, before they, too, collapsed and died. They lay in the second great mound.

"She be mighty restless," Sal said, breaking the silence.

Fergal hopped up on the bale, stretching his neck and standing on tiptoe to see.

"She's birthing," he said with such authority that I had to smother a snicker.

Kindly, none of the men insulted him by looking. But we all heard the mare sink to the deep straw bedding. How clever of animals to improve on humans in this activity. We heard several grunts from the mare, no screams or long ululating cries, no weeping and complaining about her lot, or cursing the man who brought her to this condition.

"Hooves," Fergal announced in a low voice. "Head coming. Normal position."

I couldn't keep from glancing at Dag, who winked at me, nibbling at a thick straw.

"Ah," Fergal drawled. "Just one more push, my beauty, just one little effort on your part . . . ah, there."

We heard the mare's effort, the rustle and slither on the straw, and simultaneously the suspense was too much for us. We all reached the stall at the same time, peering over the partition as the mare began to lick the placenta from her foal. The head was free and the wet little body began to struggle, the overlong legs kicking with incredible strength for a creature so newly born.

"Hey, you're blocking my view," Fergal cried. He barged in beside Dag and hung onto the partition edge to pull himself up. "What is it? What is it?"

The foal was not helping us to sex it—its legs went out at angles to its body. It snorted in disgust at its helplessness. The mare nudged its rear, the little whisk of a tail. It repositioned its legs and made another stab at rising. Its legs did not cooperate, and it gave a high-pitched little squeal of frustration. Its feet scrabbled in the straw as the foal determined to find a purchase and rise. It had skewed about now, and as it flicked its tail in annoyance, its sex was revealed. Or, to be more accurate, it revealed that it was not a female.

"A colt foal!" Fergal yelled, having paid more attention to that critical detail while we were all enchanted by the creature's sturdy independence. He flipped open the stall door and entered. "What a marvelous creature you are! What a splendid girl! What a brave mare! What a fine son you have!" Fergal stroked the mare's nose and fondled her ears, his voice rich with approval. Then he began crooning to the colt, gently smoothing the neck to get it used to human touch. The newborn was far too involved in sorting out its legs to worry about any extraneous annoyance.

"He's got a gift for 'em, he has," Pol told us, sagely nodding his head.

"Delivered three in the hill meadows all by himself after I broke my leg."

"I'll tell Alessan," I said.

"The more good news he gets, the better it'll set with him," Dag said, which struck me, as I walked quickly back up the road, as cryptic for the blunt runner handler.

When I got back to the Hall, Oklina and Desdra were gone, presumably to bed, for it was after midnight now. Tuero had propped his elbows on the table and was gesturing expansively at Alessan, who had his head down on his arms.

"That's fair enough," Tuero was saying in a

very amiable and conciliatory tone. "If a harper can't find out—and this harper is very good at finding things out—if a harper can't find out, he doesn't have the right to know. Is that right, Alessan?"

The answer was a long drawn-out snore. Tuero stared at him for a moment in mixed pity and rebuke, then pushed at the wineflask under his elbow and sighed in disgust.

"Has he finished it?" I asked, amused at the disappointment on Tuero's long face. His long, crooked-to-the-left nose twitched.

"Yes, it's empty, and he's the only one who knows where the supply is."

I smiled, remembering my trip with Oklina to the wine store. "The foal is a male, a fine strong one. I thought Lord Alessan would like to know. Dag and Fergal are watching to be sure it stands and suckles." I looked down at the sleeping Alessan, his face relaxed, peaceful. He looked younger, so much less strained. Behind the lids, did those pale green eyes still flicker with their habitual sadness?

"I know I know you," Tuero said.

"I'm not the sort of person a journeyman harper knows," I replied. "Get to your feet, Harper. I can't allow him to sleep in this uncomfortable position and he needs a proper rest."

"Not so sure I can stand."

"Try it." I am tall, but not as tall as Tuero or

Alessan, and not strong enough to shift Alessan's heavy frame by myself. I looped one lax arm over my shoulder and urged Tuero, who had managed to get upright, to take the other.

Alessan was heavy! And Tuero was not a very able assistant. He had to pull himself up the stairs by the handrail, which I sincerely prayed was firmly secured to the stonework. Fortunately, Alessan's rooms were at the head of the stairs. I hadn't been past the sitting room, still furnished with the doss-beds and bits and pieces just cast down in the press of other tasks. Tomorrow, or the next day, perhaps we could begin to freshen up the inner Hold.

I gave the heavy fur robe on Alessan's bed a yank, and it tumbled about my feet, briefly hindering us as we maneuvered Alessan's limp body. He collapsed on to the bed, feet hanging over the edge. Tuero clasped the bedpost, murmuring an apology as the bed-curtain tore a bit from its frame. I tugged off Alessan's boots, loosened his belt, bent his legs upward, and, with one hand on his hips, gave as mighty a push as I could and managed to get all of his long frame on the bed, on his right side.

"I wish . . ." Tuero began as I covered Alessan with the robe, tucking it in carefully above his shoulders so that if he rolled, he would not be cold. He smiled slightly in his sleep and my breath caught. "I wish . . ." Tuero stared at me with a suddenly blank face, frowned, and lowered his head to his chest.

"The doss-bed is still in the next room, Harper." Even with Tuero's drunken help, I doubt I could have assisted him to his room far down the corridor.

"Will you cover me up, too?"

Tuero's request was delivered in such a wistful tone that I had to smile. In two or three lurches, he had followed me into the next room. I picked up the blanket and shook it out. With a sigh of weary gratitude, he lay on his side.

"You're good to a drunken sot of a harper," he murmured as I covered him. "One day I'll re-memmmm . . ." He was unconscious. Perhaps one day Tuero would remember that it was he who had coined the phrase "the Fort Hold Horde," which had been joyfully applied to my sisters and me. I suspect it would put a blight on our relationship when he did. But that was really his problem.

Mine was getting into my own bed, and not wishing that there was someone who might care to tuck me in.

Chapter IX
3.23.43

Bright and clear, with a promise of spring that was soon to be blighted in the heart, dawned that momentous day. Despite our excesses of the night before, or because of them, we rose rested, and breakfasted early. Everyone was smiling, including Desdra, who was not much given to trivial expressions. Details of the day's business were discussed at the breakfast table. Alessan ran up to the beasthold to inspect the colt foal, expressing considerable pleasure in its strength and friskiness. Oklina and I got the fosterlings and several of the stronger male convalescents to help trundle the apprentice jars up to an unused beasthold so that some progress could be made in setting the Main Hall back to the purpose for which it was intended.

Deefer took others off to see if there might not be a few plump wherries in the hills; they would make a nice change from the tough herdbeast meat, the supply of which was now virtually exhausted.

I made plans in my head, rehearsing suggestions to present to Alessan tonight. I felt that a week's hard work would clean up the debris, and he must wish to see the last of the reminders of that horrible time. Not that we could do anything to block out the sight of the burial mounds. Spring would at least bring grass to cloak the muddy prominences. When the earth had settled, we would be able to level them, but that would be some time in the future.

"Dragons!" someone yelled from the Outer Court. We all rushed out to see the spectacle. The first one to land was B'lerion on Nabeth. Oklina's little face filled with joy. Bessera, one of the High Reaches queen riders, on her great beast, settled to the ground behind him. The Court, an ample space, seemed suddenly dwarfed and constricted by the presence of the huge beasts. They looked immensely pleased with themselves, glowing in the bright sunshine. Six more dragons, bronzes all, landed on the roadway.

As Oklina rushed out to B'lerion with his supplies, I could not help but notice the way the bronze rider's face lit up as he slipped down his dragon's side. When she reached him, she halted abruptly to gaze lovingly up at him until, smiling a trifle foolishly himself, he took the serum from her.

I felt a touch on my arm. Desdra stood there with the brace of packaged serum bottles for me to deliver to a rider. "Don't stare, Rill. It has been sanctioned."

"I wasn't staring—not exactly. But she's so young, and B'lerion has quite a reputation."

"There's a queen egg hardening at Fort Weyr."

"But Oklina's needed here."

Desdra shrugged, transferred the serum to my hands, and gave me a bit of a push to call me to attention. I rushed off, but my mind was unsettled. Oklina was so very young, and B'lerion so very charming. Yet Alessan sanctioned the alliance? How odd, when he would need her children as well to secure the Bloodline. Oh, I knew perfectly well that Ruathan women often became queen riders and that Weyrwomen conceived and bore children like any others, though not as prolifically. But I wouldn't fancy such a life. The bond between rider and dragon was too intense, too all-consuming for someone like me. What I envied in Oklina was the happiness, the rapture in her face as she looked up at B'lerion. Nabeth's rainbow-sparkling eyes were turned on the pair, as if he knew everything that was passing silently between them. Dragons had such powers, I knew. I wasn't certain I would like having someone know exactly what I was thinking all the time. But I supposed dragonriders grew accustomed to it.

No sooner had we recovered our breath from the departure of that dragon contingent than the Fort Weyr queens arrived. Leri, whom I was surprised to see, set old Holth down in the Courtyard while Kamiana, Lidora, and Haura landed on the roadway. Then S'peren and K'lon arrived. Leri was in great form, joking with Alessan and Desdra, but I noticed that she kept watching Oklina. And so did Holth. So this involvement was of recent origin? Then I remembered my arrival here at Ruatha, a mere three days ago that had the quality of three months, so much had happened in that short space. Alessan had seemed happy; so had Moreta, and Oklina had been positively shining. So was Leri reviewing the situation today?

The Weyr had the right to Search for suitable candidates from any hold, especially when a queen egg was hardening. Oklina was so young, so sweet. I chided myself for criticizing my new Lord Holder. What right had I, save that of a concerned friend? But then I was good at seeing the bad side in everything.

Around midday, we had time for a cup of soup and bread. Most of the serum bottles had been speedily delivered to the messengers—I tried to figure out the logistics of delivery. It took nearly five minutes for a dragon to land. Working as fast as we could, another five minutes were needed to hand the rider the bottles, then three to four minutes for the dragon to become airborne. Although his actual flight time *between* one location and another was a few seconds, it had to take at least half an hour to complete each delivery. With all the holds in the west, South Boll, Crom, Nabol, Fort, what few were occupied in Ruatha, Ista, and the western portions of Telgar, the entire complement of each Weyr ought to have been turned out. And there were but eight from the High Reaches, seven from Fort, and six from Ista.

"Don't try to make sense of it, Rill," Desdra advised me, her wry tone amused. "It actually can be done if one takes into account unusual draconic abilities."

Her reference confused me further, but the Istan and Fort contingents of dragons were back for their last consignments. If the dragons looked a bit off-color, that was to be expected. Going *between* must take a great deal of energy, as did all that landing and taking off. Leri looked exhausted, but then she was the oldest of the dragonriders at Fort. It was a measure of her dedication to the Weyrs that she undertook such a task.

Suddenly all the queens let out roars of angry protest. The only blue dragon present cringed. Leri looked furious, as did the other queen riders. There seemed to be an intense, if silent, conference among them. Leri signaled me, as the nearest person to her, to take her last consignment from her.

"Take these to S'peren; there's a good girl. He'll deliver."

I was soon covered in the dust stirred up by Holth's precipitous departure. I think the dragon hadn't so much as cleared the outer wall before she went *between*. A whoosh of cold air made me shudder convulsively. Everyone else had grown grim indeed when there should have been some measure of satisfaction for the completion of a difficult and most unusual task. I walked slowly back to the Hall.

"These can go back to the cool rooms." Alessan was indicating the remaining crates of serum, the extras prepared against the possibility of breakage. "We ought to get them over to Keroon Beasthold when the fuss subsides. Whoever becomes Beastcraftmaster will be glad of them. They're sure to discover more abandoned runners in Keroon or Telgar. There are many untenanted holds there now."

At that point, Deefer and his team came back, all grinning broadly, each man carrying at least one plump wherry on his back.

"We shall feast tonight. Oklina, Rill, what else can we find in the larder to add to roast wherry? We owe ourselves a real celebration; a proper meal, not another stew, and a swing round with a wineskin."

There was a general outbreak of cheers and shouts, and offers of assistance to the cooks. The Hall was enthusiastically cleared of its medical detritus, and the long-absent sturdy dinner tables were hauled, dusty, from their cupboards. They had been so hastily stored after the Gather that some still bore wine- and food-stained cloths. Oklina and I quickly bundled those up and out of sight in the mound of wash.

"I shall be sorry to leave here," Desdra said to me as she paused in collecting her bits and pieces and her records of the serum manufacture. "Despite all this—" she gestured at the disorder "—Ruatha is recovering quickly."

"You and Master Capiam must come back soon," Oklina said, her eyes still shining from B'lerion's last visit. "You'll see what Ruatha should look like, won't she, Rill?"

"Just give me elbow room, and we'll have the place to rights in no time," I vowed so fervently that Desdra laughed.

Then she winked so that Oklina wouldn't see.

"You were right to come here, Rill. You were never appreciated at your former Hold. And I'd like to apologize for misconstruing your motive in offering your assistance at the Hall. You'd've been a rare, fine help to us there."

"No, I would not have been allowed," I said, relieved that Oklina had moved out of earshot. "Here I am my own person, accepted on the strength of my own endeavors. I can be of use here, especially if Oklina—" I paused, not certain what I meant to say.

Desdra cocked one eyebrow, and I quickly corrected any misapprehension she had of high-flown ambitions.

"Oh, don't be ridiculous, Desdra. Despite Ruatha's present state, this is a prestigious Hold for alliance. Alessan's done himself no harm in anyone's eyes to pull out of this disaster with so much dignity. Every Lord Holder with eligible daughters will be courting him assiduously as soon as they can wangle conveyance here."

"You've sufficient rank, Lady Nerilka."

"Hush! Rank to be sure I *had*." I emphasized the past tense. "And little joy of it. I am far more satisfied to be part of Ruatha's future, for I had none of my own at Fort."

Desdra conceded my point with an open gesture of both hands. "Is there anyone to whom I should drop a hint of your whereabouts? I shall be most discreet."

"If you would, tell my Uncle Munchaun that you have seen me on your travels, well and happy. He'll reassure my sisters."

"Campen was worried, too, you know. He and Theskin searched the surroundings for a whole day, certain you had been hurt out gathering herbs."

I nodded, accepting what she didn't say as well as Campen's attempt.

I remember that I was wondering if we'd ever eradicate the astringent odor of redwort from the Main Hall when Oklina, setting the highly burnished copper ornaments back on the mantel, suddenly cried out and would have fallen had not Desdra, beside her, held her up. Ashen-faced, Alessan burst from the small office that had so recently been Follen's surgery.

"MORRRETTTAAA!" Alessan's scream was the anguish of a man already overburdened by grief and loss. He fell heavily to his knees after that one shout, sobs racking his body as he bent over, pounding his fists on the stone, heedless of Follen's attempts to restrain him from doing himself damage.

I couldn't stand those sobs and ran to him, kneeling so that his already-bloodied fists pummeled my thighs, not cold stone. He gripped my thighs so fiercely I had to bite my lips to suppress a cry, but then he burrowed his head in my lap, convulsed by this grief.

Moreta! What harm could have befallen her at Fort Weyr? I knew that her queen was in the Hatching Ground, surely the safest place in any Weyr.

Alessan's arms encircled my hips, his fingers clawing at my back, as he wrestled with this new and tremendous grief. I clasped him to me as tightly as I could, murmuring inanities, trying to understand what could have happened.

I was aware that Follen and Tuero were standing beside us, but whatever they said was masked by Alessan's hideous, gasping sobs and the scrape of his boots on the stone as his very body tried to escape this new tragedy.

"Whatever it is," I said, "let him purge it, for he has not indulged himself with tears until now. What can have happened to Moreta?"

"Whatever," Desdra said, joining them, "has rendered Oklina unconscious. I don't understand any of this. He's not a rider, nor is she yet."

We heard a mournful howl, far louder than could have come from the throat of only one watchwher.

"Shards!" Desdra cried.

I looked up at the anguish in her voice and saw B'lerion leaping up the stairs into the Hold, his face totally white, his eyes wild. The grayed dragon beyond him was a terribly altered Nabeth. It was his weird keening we had heard.

"Oklina!" B'lerion cried, trying to find her among us.

"She fainted, B'lerion." Desdra pointed to the Hall where Oklina's body was stretched out on the table, a servant hovering solicitously by her. "What has happened to Moreta?"

B'lerion turned haggard tear-filled eyes from Oklina to Alessan, whose sobs as he lay in my arms were as racking as ever, and the bronze rider's whole body sagged as he dropped his head on his chest. Tuero reached out to support him on one side, Follen on the other.

"Moreta went *between.*"

I couldn't quite grasp what he meant. Dragons and riders went *between* so frequently.

"On Holth. Telgar riders defected. She knew Keroon. She made the run. Holth was already tired. She did too much. They both went *between*. And died!"

I held Alessan even tighter then, my own tears mingling with his, my grief as fierce but more for him now than for the valiant Weyrwoman. How could he endure this third ghastly tragedy when he had stood so courageously against the plague, and mourned Suriana far longer than would most men. I burned anew against my father. Why, if there was any justice in the world, was Alessan so grievously assaulted by misfortunes of the most terrible degree while Tolocamp enjoyed

health, fortune, and fleshly pleasures that he no longer deserved?

I knew then why Alessan's incredible eyes had been shining the day I arrived. I certainly didn't know how Moreta and Alessan had contrived to be lovers. They could not have had much time together at all. On that afternoon, the six had been gone from Ruatha only an hour. Alessan's sanction of Oklina and B'lerion was now more comprehensible if he and Moreta were involved. I was glad that the Weyrwoman had had some joy, for I hadn't liked Sh'gall on those few times I had encountered him. He wasn't likable, whereas Moreta was. Poor Moreta. Poor, poor Alessan. What could possibly comfort him in this new trial?

Desdra had an answer. She waited until Alessan's sobbing had subsided to shudderings. Then she and Tuero lifted him from my lap. I could not move immediately, so cramped were my legs. But I could and did cushion him against my body as Desdra gently tipped a cup to his lips and told him to drink.

The look in his eyes will always haunt me: lost, totally lost, incredulous of his loss—and so, so sad. He had taken all the draught Desdra had given him, and it was merciful to him as well as to those about him that his eyelids lowered over his ghastly expression as the fellis took instant effect.

There were willing arms to transport him to his quarters, and I willing to sit by him, though Desdra assured me that she had given him enough fellis to keep him asleep until the next day.

"What can we do for him then, Desdra?" I asked, still shaken by his grief. Tears would not stop coursing down my cheeks.

"My dear Lady Nerilka, if I knew the answer to that, I would be Masterhealer." She shook her head from side to side, expressing the utter helplessness that I, too, felt to my core. "It will depend in every degree on what he will allow us to do for him. How cruel this new loss. How horribly, wastefully cruel!"

We undressed him and covered him with the fur. His face was prematurely aged, his eyes shrunken in his head, his lips drawn down, his complexion waxy-white. Desdra felt his pulse and nodded with relief. Then she sat down on the edge of the bed, wearily propping her back against the stead, her hands palms up and limp in her lap.

"He loved Moreta?" I was bold enough to ask.

Desdra nodded. "When we collected the needlethorn. What a glorious day that was!" She sighed, the faintest of smiles touching her usually austere face. "I'm glad they had that much. And perhaps, in a strange, unjust way, it is for the best. That is, if Ruatha is to endure."

"Because Alessan must secure his Bloodline?" In all of Pern's history, no Weyrwoman had become a Lady Holder, though many Lady Holders had become Weyrwomen. Moreta had been nearly to the end of safe childbearing, but Alessan could have taken a wife as well. A Lord Holder could make his own laws within his Hold, especially to secure his Bloodline. Hold girls were raised with that precept firmly implanted in their brains and hearts.

"Oklina's children were to be fostered here," Desdra said.

"But that's not enough with all his losses."

"You must tell him who you are, Lady Nerilka."

I shook my head even as I grasped firmly at the thought, at that utterly impossible possibility. He needed someone pretty and appealing, clever and charming, who could rouse him from all the grief he had endured.

She left me then, murmuring something about bringing food when it was ready. It took too much energy to tell her that I doubted I could choke anything down.

Chapter X
3. 24. 43 – 4. 23. 43

I'm not sure how any of us got
through the next few days. B'lerion stayed with
Oklina. It was more obvious than ever to me that
her destiny would be the Weyr. She had heard the
outcry from the dragons, which was unusual
enough for someone not of the Weyr or dragon-
linked. Alessan's knowledge of Moreta's death was
shatteringly unexpected to all but Desdra and
Oklina. I pieced together some parts of their story,
aided by a growing intuition that seemed to be sen-
sitive to anything concerning Alessan.

All the dragonriders and most Weyrfolk had been instantly aware of the two deaths, Moreta's and Holth's. Later B'lerion told us of the reinforced rules and disciplines imposed on all riders to prevent a recurrence of this type of tragedy.

It had begun as a logical expedient for injured riders to ask their flightworthy dragons if they would fly a sound dragonman to make up Wing strength at Threadfall. Each dragon had his own peculiarities of flight that his impressed rider understood. But, generally speaking, any dragonrider was capable of riding another's dragon. No blame could be attached to Leri for adopting that custom and allowing Moreta to ride Holth in the several emergencies that had arisen. The courtesy was by then customary Weyr practice. But tired dragons and tired riders make mistakes, and that late afternoon, Moreta and Holth had been pushed beyond mere exhaustion to the point where habit only had carried them through the motions of landing and taking off. I remembered then how Holth had gone *between* a wingspan above the Court that afternoon.

"Yes," B'lerion said, his voice a broken whisper. "Holth had lost a lot of natural spring in her hindquarters. She'd have leaped up and gone *between* before Moreta could have told her where to fly—they stayed, lost, *between*."

Later, when Master Tirone began to write a celebratory ballad about Moreta's courageous ride, Desdra told me that, at the insistence of all Weyrleaders, Moreta was to be properly mounted on her own queen, not Holth. To broadcast the truth behind that tragedy could have done incalculable harm. Most of Pern never knew the truth. I'm not so certain I was all that glad to be in the minority. Not that it diminished Moreta's heroism in my estimation, but because so simple a mistake was causing so much anguish.

Desdra also told me, since she knew me to be discreet and trustworthy, how the dragonriders had managed to make so many deliveries. This had contributed to their total exhaustion, a major factor in the tragedy: Dragons could go as easily *between* one time and another as one place to another. Moreta and Holth had overtaxed their strength in this way. For only by stretching time in this bizarre fashion, or rather doubling back on themselves, could Moreta and Holth manage to deliver serum to all the holds on the Keroon plains. Moreta had been the only one of the riders available that fateful day sufficiently familiar with Keroon's many half-hidden holds to have succeeded in that task.

Telgar Weyr was to suffer disciplinary action from the other Weyrs, led by Weyrwomen. They were unalterably convinced that had M'tani not been so intransigent and permitted his riders to fly, Moreta's life would not have been lost. I never did learn what was done against Telgar Weyr. If Oklina ever knew, she never mentioned it.

I also was now in a far better way of understanding how the six people—Alessan, Moreta, Capiam, Desdra, Oklina, and B'lerion—had spent that hour preceding my arrival at Ruatha. I had previously assumed that supplies of needlethorn had been available, not that these six courageous people had dared to spend a whole day in the future harvesting the thorns on far Ista.

I understood a great deal—yet it was not enough to help Alessan. I knew only that I wondered how he would find the courage to continue after this latest brutal tragedy.

He came back to consciousness, and awareness of this new sorrow, twenty-four hours later. I had been dozing, and roused at the slight sound his restlessness occasioned. I had to look away from his haunted, almost wild eyes.

"Desdra drugged me?" When I nodded, my own eyes downcast, he cursed her. "It won't help. Nothing will help. Does anyone know what happened?"

So I told him, somehow able to keep my voice level and calm though my throat kept closing up. The waves of grief that rolled from the man were palpable. He stared at me when I had finished, eyes burning in his drained white face.

"But Leri and Orlith could go together!" His

resentment and fury were compressed into that accusation.

"The eggs. Orlith stays until they hatch, Leri with her."

"Brave Leri! Gallant Orlith!" His sarcasm made me flinch, but the agony in his rigid body, his clenched fists, told me that a different struggle was being fought. "Dragons and riders have many advantages denied us! Would that my father had released me on that Search! When I consider how much different my life would have been . . ." He turned away from me, his face toward the window. Then, because I knew his view included the burial mounds, I knew why he turned back, his shadowed eyes closed in the taut skin of his tormented face.

"So you have watched me while I slept, loyal Rill. And I shall have a new guardian, no doubt, whenever I wake, to keep me living a life I have no wish to live."

My own anguish spoke then, not the sensible, patient, dutiful, plain member of the Fort Hold Horde, but Suriana's friend, Alessan's newest holder, and someone who valued him far more than she should. Any sorrow may be borne. Time will heal the deepest hurt of heart—but time must be won.

"You may not want to live, Lord Holder of Ruatha, but you don't have the right to die!"

"Ruatha is no longer sufficient reason for me

to live!" he told me in a bitter, intense, angry voice. "It's tried to kill me once already."

"And you have fought to save it. No one else could have done so much, with so much honor and dignity."

"Honor and dignity mean nothing in the grave!" He flung his arm up, toward the window and the graves of so many.

"You still breathe, and you are Ruatha." I spoke sharply, wondering if anything I said could jolt him out of the course he had tacitly announced. Duty and honor and tradition were such cold substitutes for a beautiful woman and her love. "As your holder, Lord Alessan, I require that you have an heir of your Blood to leave behind you." I surprised myself with the vehemence in my voice, and he frowned as he looked up at me. "Unless you want Fort or Tillek or Crom Blood to hold Ruatha at your defection. Then I'll mix the fellis for you myself and you can quit!"

"A bargain, then." With a quickness I hadn't expected from a man lying abed so wracked and spent with grief, he was upright, extending an implacable hand to me. "When you are with child, Nerilka, I'll drink that cup."

I stared back at him, aghast that my rallying words had evoked such a response from him, stunned that he misconstrued what I had said and applied it personally to me. Then I realized that he knew my name.

"Your parents have always favored an alliance
. . ." His words were derisive, sneering.

"Not me, Alessan, not me."

"Why not you, Nerilka? You've shown all the
qualities of the perfectly trained Lady Holder.
Why else are you so fortuitously at Ruatha? Or
did you think to revenge those deaths on me?"

"Oh, no! No! I could no longer endure Fort.
Tolocamp sunk himself beneath contempt. How
could I remain there when he denied the healers
medicine and help. Coming here was chance. I
was at Bestrum's when M'barak came and asked
for help. How can you know who I am?"

"Suriana." Then, more irritably, he said, "You
fostered with her, Rill. You know how endlessly
she sketched. Your face appeared in many drawings. How could I not know Nerilka when we
finally meet? What I didn't know was why you'd
come, so I let you have your anonymity." Then
he snapped his fingers impatiently. "Come, girl,
it is not so bad a bargain, to be undisputed Lady
Holder of Ruatha, and no Lord to abuse you for-
ever. You can't be afraid of me? I never beat Suriana. Surely she told you that I was a good husband to her."

She had told me that, not in so many words,
but implying much more than goodness, but the
thought of her now dead, and of his so palpable
grief for Moreta, made the tears flow down my
cheeks again.

"You are kind and good and brave, and do not deserve to be so ill used by circumstance."

"I seem unable to avoid misfortunes, Nerilka." His voice was harsh, his face coldly set. "Spare me your pity. I have no use for it. Give me instead the child to carry on Ruathan Blood? And the cup?"

How I could have agreed to either part of the bizarre bargain I now wonder, but at the time I thought that surely when the worst of his grief had passed, Alessan would reconsider taking the cup even if I could find the courage to mix it. I would have said anything at that moment.

"Then let us begin the first now." His hand compelled me to the bed, but I broke his grip, horrified, not entirely by his precipitous behavior.

"No, I will not imitate Anella."

Alessan regarded me with angry incomprehension.

"Tolocamp had Anella in his bed an hour after he knew my mother was dead."

"Our circumstances are vastly different, Nerilka." His expression was terrible, his eyes now burning.

"You loved Moreta."

A muscle in his cheek twitched and his eyes stared coldly at me, glittering with something so akin to hatred that I recoiled.

"Is that what holds you back, Lady Nerilka?

I'd liefer it be maidenly modesty. I never knew a Fortian to go back on his word."

He taunted me and, exerting pressure on my hand, drew me inexorably to him. I tried to put in words any one of the many reasons why I resisted him then, the main of which was that this was such an inauspicious moment for a proceeding that was reputed to delight the participants.

"A man who has tasted death needs loving to remind him of life, Nerilka." Now his voice was persuasive, and I was very close to capitulation when we both heard the scrape of the outer door and quiet footfalls.

"You are reprieved, Nerilka, but not for long," he said in a swift, low, intense tone. "We have made a bargain—Lord and holder—and it will be consummated, the sooner the better. I long for that cup."

Tuero entered quietly, relief on his kind, long face when he saw that Alessan was awake and talking to me. "Were you wanting anything, Alessan?"

"My clothes," Alessan said, holding out his hand for them. I got clean ones from the press, and Tuero handed him his boots. He dressed quickly, then led us from his room.

If his appearance was a surprise to those in the Hall, his manner was even more of a shock. He collected Deefer, sent a fosterling for Dag, wanted to know where Oklina was, and did not question Desdra's continued presence when she and Oklina arrived together. But he turned sharply away when Oklina reached to embrace him, and sharply requested that Tuero and I join the others in his office. Then, in a low, controlled, but uninflected voice, he told us what must now be accomplished as quickly and thoroughly as possible.

Everyone was so grateful to see him plunge into activity that no one but I knew that he was setting Ruatha Hold in order for his death. Not content with physical labor, he spent long hours at night with Tuero, sending out messages, some by drum but others in sealed letters conveyed by mounted messengers. I could hear the first—requests for brood mares for his stallions, requests for any holdless families with good reputations to apply to him. Some of the messages were reminders of marks owed Ruatha Hold; I saw those entries in the Records. He sent everyone able to walk or ride out to check on the condition of the empty holds, to tally what stock remained in the fields and in what condition, to discover what crops had been sown and their progress.

I, for one, found no joy in the work, colored as it was by his cheerlessness and dispassionate industry. We had worked harder making the serum, but a strong and good spirit had imbued us then. Now there was no animation in any of us, as if Alessan's emotionlessness drained us as

well. There was even scant satisfaction in seeing
Ruatha refurbished and clean, every removable
evidence of the epidemic cleared away. Oklina
put spring flowering plants about the Hall, hoping to cheer us up. Some of them withered and
died immediately, as if they, too, could not survive
in this atmosphere. I worried constantly that
what I had said to Alessan had been wrong, that
I had brought about this fearful change in him
by appearing to condone his desired suicide.

Ten days after Moreta's death, at our somber
evening meal, Alessan got to his feet, command-
ing our instant attention. He took a thin roll from
his belt.

"Lord Tolocamp permits me to take his daughter, Lady Nerilka, as my wife," he announced in
his blunt, uninflected way.

Much later, I came across that roll, wedged in
the back of a coffer. Tolocamp's actual words
were: "If she is there, take her. She is no longer
kin of mine." Alessan need not have spared my
feelings; but it proved in yet another way that an
essential goodness of spirit was imprisoned behind that emotionless facade.

That evening there was a ripple of surprise,
but no one looked at me. Not even Tuero. Desdra
had returned to the Healer Hall five days before.

"Lady Nerilka?" Oklina asked timidly, staring
with wide eyes at her brother.

"The Ruathan Bloodline must continue," Alessan went on, and then gave a mirthless snort. "Rill agrees to that."

Everyone looked at me then as I stared straight ahead.

"I remember now where I've seen you before," Tuero began. He smiled, the first smile I had seen in the ten days. "Lady Nerilka." He rose, bowing to me amid the scattered gasps of surprise.

Oklina stared only one moment longer, and then she was around the table, her arms about me, crying and trying not to cry. "Oh, Rill. Is it really you?"

"I have received permission from her Lord Holder. We have a harper present and sufficient witnesses, so the agreement can be formalized."

"Surely not just like that?" Oklina protested, snapping her fingers.

I took her hand in mine, pressing it firmly. "Just like this, Oklina." With my eyes, I begged her not to protest. "There is too much to be done to waste time, or marks that we don't have, on ceremony."

She allowed herself to be persuaded, but her little face was troubled. For my sake, I know. So I stood up, and Alessan took me by the hand, and we faced the assembled. He took a gold marriage mark from his pouch and repeated the formal request that I become his Lady Holder and wife, mother of his issue and honored before all others in Ruatha Hold. I took the mark—later I would see that it had been engraved with the day's date—and told him that I accepted the honor to become his Lady Holder and wife, though it was hard for me to add, "mother of his issue and honored before all others." But that was our bargain.

Oklina insisted on wine, the effervescent white of Lemos, so that all could toast our union. The traditional words were spoken by a harper who could not smile and had no new song to celebrate the occasion. The handshakes I received were firm, and one or two of the women were tearful, but it was a grim wedding day. Remembering that I was a bride, I managed to smile.

Tuero presented the Family Record for us to inscribe our names, my Bloodline, and the date, then Alessan excused us.

He was kind, and very gentle, and it broke my heart to sense how mechanical he was about the business.

Not much else changed, for I would not be treated formally and remained Rill to everyone. Uncle Munchaun sent me the jewels I had left with him, along with a small but heavy chest of marks. These were my dower. He also told me what Tolocamp had said when he learned of my whereabouts: "Ruatha Hold swallows all my women, and if Nerilka prefers Ruathan hospitality to mine, this is the end of her as my daughter."

Uncle told me this because he wanted me to

hear it from him. But Uncle thought I had done exceedingly well for myself, and he wished me good fortune. I could have wished that good fortune were as visible as jewels and marks so I could display it to Alessan. Uncle added with great satisfaction that Anella had been infuriated by the news, having been certain that I was hiding in a sulk somewhere in the Hold. Finally she had complained bitterly about my continued absence to Tolocamp, who, indeed, hadn't realized I was missing until that moment.

Holdless men, their families crowded into wheeled carts or drays, arrived in a fairly steady stream. Oklina and I fed them and let the women wash in the bathing rooms, managing to establish certain standards and values about them. Tuero, Dag, Pol, Sal, and Deefer would chat up the men over a cup of klah or a bowl of soup. Follen would give them a once-over for health and fitness. Strangely enough, it was often Fergal who would have the final telling word, and to whom Alessan listened most acutely. He gleaned information from the children that sometimes did not tally with what the adults had said. Always to our advantage.

We were fortunate enough to attract younger sons of lateral Bloodlines from Keroon, Telgar, Tillek, and the High Reaches, so that the Hold once again filled its empty apartments and there were more capable supervisors. Craftsmen were sent, approved by Mastercraftsmen, with tools and supplies. Now, when I walked up the cot line to the beastholds, there were cheerful greetings from the settled, happy women, and children playing on the dancing square and in the meadows before lessons with Tuero. Gradually our subdued and somber meals took on some semblance of relaxation and geniality. That lasted until we heard from M'barak, who frequently was on convey duty to Ruatha Hold, that the Hatching was imminent.

Then all of us were reminded of Moreta, Leri, and Orlith—and Oklina. I was horribly reminded of my bargain with Alessan. It was too soon to know if his attention to me was successful: that was the only alleviating factor for the stress I was obliged to hide from everyone.

Though Alessan never spoke about the Impression, we had come to assume that Oklina would be permitted to take her place among the candidates for the queen egg. We all knew that B'lerion came on more visits than the tactful ones he made by way of the Court.

I was dumbfounded when Alessan asked me had I a gown suitable for the Hatching.

"You cannot want to go?"

"Want, no! But the Lord and Lady of Ruatha will not absent themselves from *this* Hatching. Oklina deserves our support!" The look on his face chided me that I could even for a moment consider any other course. He was grimy with travel, for he had ridden far to settle the new occupants of one of the pasture holds. "Look through the chests in my mother's room. She always had fabrics put by. You're too tall to fit anything already made." A shadow crossed his face, and he quickly went to bathe.

He came to me every night, kind and thorough, until the morning when we both knew I had not yet conceived. I cannot tell you how relieved I was, that feeling overpowering any sense of failure that I had not immediately conceived for him, for it meant he must live another month at least. I would have that much more of his company to remember. I could no longer deny to myself that Alessan had always been important to me from the moment he had married my dear Suriana, just as Ruatha had been the haven denied me first by the circumstance of her death, and then by my parents' arbitrary decision at Gathertime. Now he was vital to my heart and soul in a way that I never could have anticipated in the wildest flight of fancy. I treasured every casual touch; sometimes, in the night, I would feel his questing hand, as if to reassure his sleeping self that I was still there. I cherished each word he spoke of approval for my management, my suggestions. I stored them up, as others might hoard marks or harvests, to strengthen me in the famine of his absence.

I admit that as Oklina and I, along with two of the new women who professed some skill with their needles, sewed the dress out of the soft red fabric, I sewed with a lighter heart than I had had in recent days. Oklina had made her white candidate's shift quietly in her room in the evenings so as not to distress anyone. When we women sewed together, she began to chatter, giving me bits and pieces of Hold history, even anecdotes from Suriana's all-too-brief time here. She knew by now that it did not distress me to talk of my foster sister. Indeed, I welcomed the opportunity to mention my beloved friend. No one at Fort Hold had been the least interested in my fostering days, or in hearing about a girl whom none of them had met.

Gradually, I rediscovered pleasure in Ruatha, in building the new foundations, in welcoming new holders and settling them. We practiced every economy, of which I contributed my own share by way of that chest of marks and the management I had learned from my lady mother. The Hold was desperately shy of many staple supplies, not only foodstuffs. The Healer Hall graciously reimbursed Ruatha for, I believe the accompanying note said, the labor and raw materials used in the serum.

Alessan ground his teeth, but altruism feeds and supplies no one. We didn't have to argue with him to accept the very modest income for what his honor had prompted him to do. Those marks allowed us to buy equipment, to commission plows, cart frames, and wheels from the Mastersmith, and bare necessities from other Crafthalls. Every item supplied had to be credited against the individual holder's accounts with us. I spent as much time in the evenings on my Records now as Alessan did on his. We worked together in what became a companionable silence, broken when Oklina came in with the small supper meals. I saw occasional signs of his relaxing just a little. Then something, external or internal, would return him to that terrible, sad isolation.

Chapter XI

4. 23. 43

T*he drums warned us that riders* were coming to collect us. B'lerion came for Oklina, bringing a magnificent fur cloak to protect her from the chill of *between*. Oklina, Alessan, and I, all in fine new clothes, met him on the steps of the Hold as he formally requested Oklina in Search. With equal but emotionless and silent formality, Alessan nodded acceptance of the Search and placed Oklina's hand in B'lerion's.

I saw tears in the bronze rider's eyes, and then Oklina flung her arms about her brother's neck, sobbing. Alessan stiffly unwound her arms and almost pushed her at B'lerion. His face was stony as B'lerion wordlessly led Oklina away. I knew how hard it must have been for Alessan, and bowed my head against this fresh onslaught of despair.

A red-eyed M'barak arrived to escort us to Fort Weyr, and I quailed, knowing the reason for such tears. It was Alessan who showed me the courage to face the inevitable.

Hatchings are supposed to be joyous days, since Impression celebrates the beginning of brave new partnerships between dragons and men and women. How today's Impression at Fort Weyr could possibly contain any element of joy, I could not guess. And arriving at Fort Weyr was even more horrific. All the dragonriders were red-eyed, all the dragons a trifle gray-hued. All the guests were subdued, though not all of them knew that Leri and Orlith had gone *between* at dawn.

Despite the numbers of people arriving, despite their gay and festive garb, there was no conversation, no murmur of pleasantries as we all trudged across the Bowl and into the Hatching Ground. I hoped the somber mood would not affect the dragonets, or have some other unforeseen adverse effect. I don't think I could have sustained another disappointment; I marveled once more at Alessan's great strength of character and purpose.

So I held firm to the knowledge that if we survived this ghastly day, I would have Alessan's company for another month. I had to hold on to positive matters. I had to hold on to dignity and honor to sustain me in this day of crisis. I had to remember that I was now Lady Holder of Ruatha Hold, one of the oldest Holds in Pern, and that our sister was a candidate for the queen egg. I had the right to be proud today. So I held myself tall and proud beside Alessan and wished with all my heart that his courage would be sufficient to see him through the day.

He was pale, I noticed in a quick sideways glance, but pride must have strengthened him, too. As we entered the Hatching Ground itself, he courteously took my arm. I was as glad for his support, for it was difficult to maintain any dignity while hot sands burned through the thin soles of my light shoes. Alessan led me to the tiers on the far left of the Ground. When we were seated, he kept his eyes studiously on the eggs, focusing in particular on the golden egg slightly apart from the others on a raised mound of sand.

I looked about me, because I could not look at the eggs or at Alessan. Master Capiam was there, blowing his nose fiercely, and the newly created Masterhealer, Desdra, sat beside him, looking sad, proud, and anxious all at once. Desdra would not be returning to her former Hall, as had been her original intention on attaining her Mastery. She was remaining with Capiam, and I so hoped that meant what I thought it might.

Masterharper Tirone and a huge number of harpers of various ranks were just arriving, so I didn't miss the entrance of Tolocamp and the gaudily dressed little Anella. She looked over the tiers and then pulled Tolocamp off to one side, distancing herself from us, I'd no doubt. The other Weyrleaders and Weyrwomen filed in, though Falga limped badly crossing the sands. Someone behind me pointed out the Benden Lord and his lady and the major Lords Holder as they entered. That was the first time, I think, that I realized I now held equal rank with such famous folk. Ratoshigan entered by himself, as usual. Craftmasters and their ladies arrived, although I saw few visitors with the Telgar Badge; many were wearing Keroon's.

Then I heard the humming, which grew in excitement as the dragons, gripped by a sense of occasion, sang a welcome to the candidates. Sh'gall himself led in the four girls, then fussily motioned for the boys to walk on while he positioned the girls in front of the queen egg. Other eggs were beginning to rock, and the dragons' song became ecstatic. My heart began to lift, my pulses quickened. Oh, please, let it be Oklina!

That would be the best sign there could be that our sorrows, Ruathan sorrows, were over.

She stood there so proudly, no more a shy, uncertain, slender girl, but a confident, dignified young lady. I had tears in my eyes. I had unconsciously clenched my hands into fists when I felt Alessan's hand unclasp one, his cold fingers lacing into mine.

One egg, just below us, began to rock strongly. Others were equally agitated, and I could hear people behind me make wagers as to which egg would crack first. I wouldn't have won; the egg below us broke and a moist dragon head appeared, crooning piteously as the dragonet shook itself free of the shell. It was a bronze! A sigh of relief rose from every throat. It was a very good sign for a bronze to be the first to hatch. The little beast staggered directly toward a tallish boy with a shock of light brown hair. That was also a good sign, that the dragonet knew whom he wanted. The boy didn't quite believe it and looked in appeal to his neighbors. With a laugh, they gave him a push toward the lumbering dragonet. No longer resisting such good fortune, the boy ran to kneel in the sand before the little bronze and stroke his head.

Tears were streaming down my face now, and I was hardly the only one so affected. No one could fault me for such a display. I had not realized that I had bottled up so many tears inside.

To cry was to release all sorts of ugly little pressures and tensions. Like waking out of a long, dark dream to a sun-filled day. Then I saw through the mist of tears, with Alessan holding my hand tightly, that a blue had found his chosen partner. The hum of the mature dragons was augmented by the crooning trill of the hatchlings and the excited exclamations of the newly chosen riders and their happy relatives in the tiers.

Suddenly everyone had eyes only for the queen egg, which was rocking violently. As Alessan's fingers crushed mine, I realized that he cared about the outcome of this far more than he would permit himself to hope—if only because expressing hope or love or care of anything must, in his lexicon, mean its loss. That flash of perception gave me the insight and knowledge to persevere in our relationship, and to understand the man who appeared to everyone else as undemonstrative and uncaring.

Then the egg gave three good wobbles and cracked neatly in half, the fragments falling away from the little queen who seemed to spring from the shards. Another positive omen!

Two girls wavered in their stance. I heard Alessan catch his breath, but I was filled with a strange and overpowering certainty which girl the little queen would choose. Quickly and with considerably more agility than the rest of the clutch had shown, the moistly gold queen made

straight for Oklina. I didn't know that I had started to cling to Alessan, but his arm encircled me as Oklina lifted shining eyes, her gaze instinctively finding B'lerion.

"Her name is Hannath!" Oklina cried in a voice of exultation and amazement, her face so radiant that she was truly beautiful.

"Oh, Alessan! Alessan! Alessan!" I kept repeating, clinging to him, unwilling to express the tumultuous joy in my heart, but equally unable to suppress it even when I knew how painful this scene must be for him.

"She knew Oklina would Impress," he said in a broken voice, staring down at Oklina's glowing face. I knew he was speaking of Moreta. "She knew!" He clung to me then, his grip so fierce I could not breathe. I felt the anguish in his body, the pounding of his heart. Then his chest heaved in one massive sob, and he buried his face in my shoulder, sagging against me for the support I gladly gave him. Was this the reason I had been made so tall? We stood like that only a few moments, then parted, Alessan sinking to the seat and looking out across the Sands. I know he saw nothing, for he made no sign when B'lerion and Oklina looked at us. I signaled them that we would follow. Then everyone else left.

The silence in the Hatching Ground was profound, the excitement outside in the Bowl muted by the great stone walls. Finally Alessan raised his head, gazing across the sands to the tiers on the other side. His manner had altered in a subtle way I could not then explain. It was as if he had let go, as perhaps he had at that moment of Impression for Oklina. Had he ended grief as she began a new life? Could he find a new life, too?

"I gave her back her Gather gown there." His voice was a whisper I had to strain to hear. "She gave me hope and help. I can never forget her, Rill."

"None of us should, Alessan."

He had not wept, though his eyes were red and his face blotchy. He wiped my cheeks dry, as Uncle Munchaun often had. He didn't smile, but he didn't look so stonily hard of eye and mouth. He rose then and stepped to the next level down, holding up his hand to me.

"Today is Oklina's joy day. Nothing, not even old sorrow, should mar it. Nor, honorable Rill, will I require that cup of you." We had started down the tiers and he was watching his steps, so he did not see how near I came to tears again with this new pressure of joy in my heart. "There is too much to be done at Ruatha, now we have lost Oklina to the Weyr. I could not have stood in her way as my father did in mine. Now I am relieved that I did not. I had to come to Fort Weyr to understand that lives end, and lives begin."

"Oh, Alessan."

We were on the hot sands again, and since I

didn't have to be on my dignity in front of a critical audience, I grabbed his hand and began to run. I had to do something active with relief boiling about inside me. "My feet are burning, and we mustn't be too tardy in our congratulations."

With a noise that was almost a laugh, Alessan followed me out of the Hatching Ground and toward the festivities already begun in Fort Weyr's Bowl. Above us, outlined against the brilliant sky, dragons crowded every available perching space on the Rim. And the sun made a gold of every one of them.

Chapter XII

3. 11. 1553 Interval

*A*s *I conclude this narrative, there*
has been no Thread to blot our skies for five marvelous Turns. Few signs remain of what Ruatha
endured, for the burial mounds have been leveled
and their sites are all but invisible in the luxurious
grass.

And change, the change from unrelenting
Thread, has benefited all. Kamiana is Weyrwoman at Fort, and G'drel, a genial, heavyset
man originally of Telgar, is Weyrleader. His Do-
rianth flew Pelianth on her next mating flight.

No one hears much of Wingleader Sh'gall these days, but G'drel and Kamiana are often visitors here, and G'drel constantly teases Alessan about his runner, Squealer. He's about the only one, save Fergal, who dares, even though Alessan is generally easier to approach on most matters.

B'lerion's Nabeth outmaneuvered every bronze on Pern to fly Oklina's Hannath, not that anyone doubted the outcome of that flight. Her two sons now play with ours, for I have fulfilled the first half of my original bargain with Alessan five times: four strong sons and a daughter whom we have named Moreta. Alessan will not have me overbear, though I keep telling him that I am happiest pregnant and never suffer as others have from being in that condition.

He is even permitting himself to show affection to his children. At first he pretended total indifference, as if any tenderness would mark them as victims for disaster. To my delight, they have been incredibly healthy, less prone to catch the usual childhood maladies than any other children of the Hold, sturdily immune to cuts, bruises, and breaks that often occur in childhood. Our daughter, Moreta—and Desdra has told me quite sincerely that she is the most beautiful child she ever saw, so it is not only this doting mother who so describes her—has provided the sun to thaw the coldness in her father. He could not help but adore her, for she seems to blossom with joy whenever she sees him, and her delight is contagious. Alessan will never be as carefree, blithe, or gay as Suriana described him, but his smile is readier now, and he will laugh at Tuero's outrageous humor and smile at his sons' antics and boasts. He will cheer when Squealer wins yet another race and be a genial host when visitors are in the Hall.

We plan our first Gather, a very modest affair, when the spring has dressed the land with blossom and new growth. If occasionally when we make our plans, a shadow crosses Alessan's face, it is to be expected, and I ignore it.

If he does not love me as he did Suriana or Moreta, still he loves me in ways he would not have known with his first wild and tempestuous wife and different from his deep devotion to Moreta. We understand each other well, often starting the same sentence simultaneously. Certainly we are of similar mind in every matter concerning Ruatha Hold and our children. He is public in his appreciation of my efforts, though he cannot know that his ready acknowledgment of my efforts is the greatest of compliments he could pay me, the girl who was never praised or thanked by her own Blood.

And gradually, as his fear of losing yet again that which is precious to him abates, his regard has extended to all areas of our life together. At night it is not the shadow of Suriana or the dream

of Moreta that he holds in his arms and loves—
it is Nerilka, his wife, the mother of his children,
and the Lady of his Hold.

It is time to end a story that began in sorrow
and ordeal and has ended in a deep and lasting
happiness. May it be so for others.

Appendix

The illustrations in this appendix were based on maps drawn by Karen Wynn Fonstad for *The Atlas of Pern* (Del Rey/Ballantine Books, 1984).

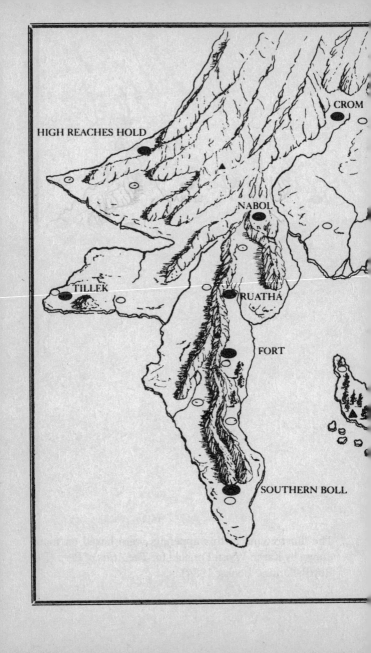

CROM

HIGH REACHES HOLD

NABOL

TILLEK

RUATHA

FORT

SOUTHERN BOLL

ELGAR

LEMOS

BITRA

BENDEN

IGEN

KEROON

NERAT

▲ WEYR

⬤ MAJOR HOLD

◯ LESSER HOLD

PERN–NORTHERN CONTINENT

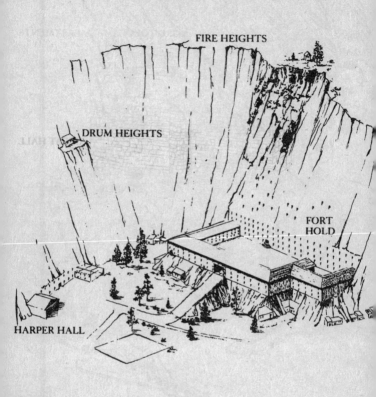

FIRE HEIGHTS

DRUM HEIGHTS

FORT
HOLD

HARPER HALL

FORT HOL

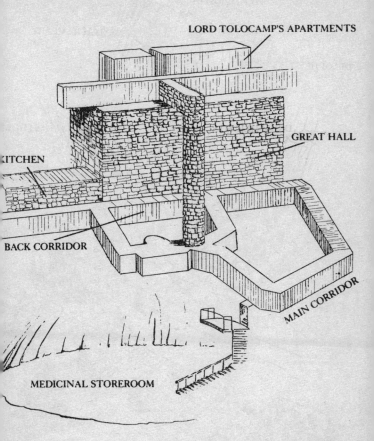

LORD TOLOCAMP'S APARTMENTS

GREAT HALL

KITCHEN

BACK CORRIDOR

MAIN CORRIDOR

MEDICINAL STOREROOM

INTERIOR OF FORT HOLD

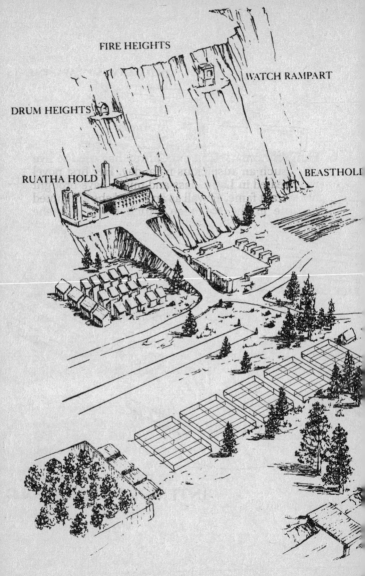

FIRE HEIGHTS

WATCH RAMPART

DRUM HEIGHTS

RUATHA HOLD

BEASTHOLD

RUATH

About the Author

Born on April 1, Anne McCaffrey has tried to live up to such an auspicious natal day. Her first novel was created in Latin class and might have brought her instant fame, as well as an A, had she attempted to write in the language. Much chastened, she turned to the stage and became a character actress, appearing in the first successful summer music circus at Lambertville, New Jersey. She studied voice for nine years and, during that time, became intensely interested in the stage direction of opera and operetta, ending this phase of her life with the stage direction of the American premiere of Carl Orff's *Ludus De Nato Infante Mirificus*, in which she also played a witch.

By the time the three children of her marriage were comfortably at school most of the day, she had already achieved enough success with short stories to devote full time to writing.

Between her frequent appearances in the United States and England as a lecturer and guest-of-honor at science-fiction conventions, Ms. McCaffrey lives at Dragonhold, in the hills of Wicklow County, Ireland, with two cats, two dogs, and assorted horses. Of herself, Ms. McCaffrey says, "I have green eyes, silver hair, and freckles; the rest changes without notice."